I'm Not My Father

Damian Myron

Myron, Damian. I'm Not My Father

Thursday

1: Morning Routine

Cal did a cursory flip through his folder to doublecheck he had everything with him before he left.

Advanced calculus homework: Check.

Rough draft of his Civil War paper with at least five references: Check.

Notes for the presentation he had to give for Senior Spanish, a class which few juniors besides himself were taking: Check.

He slid the folder into his bookbag with a satisfied smile. The only thing he had left to do was write a one-page current events essay for the state-mandated class Participation in Government. That was going to be easy enough.

Enjoyable, even.

Cal tiptoed out of his bedroom so as not to disturb his parents, though when he noticed their bedroom door was slightly ajar, he peeked through the sliver of an opening. The door to their master bathroom was shut, but it did nothing to mute the whirring of the bathroom fan. His mother lay alone, face sunk deep into a pillow. Half the sheets were dangling over the edge of the bed, suggesting another restless night, though she lay motionless now. The last few months had been hard on her. Cal decided to let her rest in peace.

He crept down the carpeted hallway into the kitchen, taking care not to cause too much of a ruckus as he prepared breakfast. A bottle of vodka was tucked behind the English muffins in the breadbasket. That was a new hiding spot.

He contemplated stuffing it in his bag to bring to a party over the weekend, but didn't want to risk some teacher spotting him with it and making the last months before summer a living hell for him.

Instead, he opened the fridge and buried it under a heap of vegetables that had been neglected all month. There was a good chance the bottle would still be found and emptied before he returned home, but if it wasn't, he could still play the hero for the rest of his underage partygoers.

While he burned the English muffins to his liking, he pulled a notebook out of his bag and flipped on a portable TV stationed on the counter, spun the dial all the way down to mute, but feared the damage had already been done as a sportscaster screeched about another Sox loss the moment the TV sprang to life. He snapped his neck back down the hallway, expecting his father to come stampeding through the door. His father's wrath (a generous description) didn't faze him.

It was his mother he was concerned about.

Cal stood there, waiting. All he could hear was the bathroom fan running. And the muffins popping out of the toaster.

They didn't hear it.

Cal plucked the muffin halves out of the toaster, slathered thick gobs of butter over them, poured himself some cereal (after checking behind each box for a bottle, because that's where he *usually* found them), slowly raised the volume on the TV until the words were just above a whisper, and settled in to listen to the latest developments.

The image on the TV screen cut back to local news anchors. Along the side of the screen was a rundown of the stories they were covering next. The side of his mouth crooked into a smile when Cal saw which story topped the list. He shoveled a spoonful of cereal into his mouth to keep from salivating.

"*New details have emerged this morning in the saga of a small town's biggest mystery,*" the lead anchor whispered through the television. "*We now go live—*"

The image cut to a trailer park on the outskirts of town. Cal's attention dropped momentarily as he tried to guess what the latest revelation could be about.

"What are you doing?"

Cal jumped in his seat, dropping his spoon into the nearly overflowing bowl of cereal. Some of the milk splashed over the lip of the porcelain vessel, carrying some flakes overboard with them.

He placed a hand on his chest, hoping to ease his pounding heart. Cal didn't think he was easy to startle, but three things had led to the well-executed jump scare. The words hadn't been whispered, but snapped at him. They hadn't come from the TV, but behind him. And, the voice belonged to his

"*Dad!*" Cal growled angrily as he turned to find his father standing in the kitchen door that led to their backyard.

He regarded the man with a look of betrayal, believing his father to have still been in the bathroom, when in fact, Milo must have just forgotten to turn off the fan before leaving the house for his usual morning walk. Cal sheepishly looked away from him, averting his eyes back to the counter, where the flakes looked like buoys wading in a puddle.

"Look what you made me do," Cal said hotly as he rose to fetch some paper towels. "What are you doing sneaking around like that?"

His words angered him more as he recalled that, not too long ago, *he* was sneaking around the house, hoping to avoid detection.

"Turn that off," Milo said, pointing at the TV.

Cal tore away a few squares of paper towels and stole a glance at the TV. From where he stood, he couldn't hear anything the field reporter was saying, even if Milo wasn't talking. His best chance at ~~salvaging~~ learning the latest developments would be to piece it together by the images that were being broadcast on TV. So far, they were still showing live footage of the mobile homes.

"Dad, it's for a school assignment," Cal protested.

Milo shook his head. "You know the rules."

He did. He'd agreed to them. The rational side of Cal's head, which he prided himself on, knew he didn't have a leg to stand on in this argument. But his emotional side wanted a fight. It had wanted to channel his anger toward his father for some time now, he admitted to himself.

"I know, but Dad, I have to write about current events. That means turning on the news. I have no control over what stories they cover."

Cal turned his eyes back to the TV. Still footage of the trailer parks. He pressed himself to think what the story could be about. His first thought was something about Morris, but he dismissed that quickly. Morris hadn't lived on that side of town for at least a decade now.

"Then change the channel," Milo said.

Cal could tell the bile was riding up in his father, even though his voice remained calm and level. He snorted at the suggestion's absurdity. "You think the other channels aren't giving constant up—"

"It doesn't matter," Milo said, with a shake of his head. "We agreed we weren't going to be following that story under this roof."

Cal sneered at his father. "So, if I moved the TV outside the front door, could I watch it then?" he shot back, indulging himself in his unbridled teenage need to challenge authority. He winced at the way his words made him feel like a five-year-old throwing a tantrum until he got his way.

"*You,*" Milo said, making a point to emphasize the word, "agreed it might be difficult hearing those awful things about people we know around town." Milo still kept his voice calm.

For a moment, Cal believed Milo was only doing so in the hopes he would not wake Cal's mother, until he remembered his father wasn't much for shouting matches even when she was awake. Cal had noted they'd retreated behind their bedroom door a lot in the past few months in the hopes that the two inches of wood would hide their arguments from Cal. The oak may have been successful shielding Cal's ears from Milo's yells, but Cal imagined his mother's shouts went unanswered, picturing Milo just sitting at the edge of their bed, taking the brunt of his wife's scorn.

Cal's eyes danced back to the screen, memorizing every detail of the mobile home. He was willing to settle for describing it to Zell and asking if he knew who would've owned that home, when the image changed to a woman wearing a baseball hat that had probably been haggard when she'd received it as a hand-me-down, being interviewed. Cal searched through his encyclopedic knowledge of everyone involved in this story and couldn't place her.

Milo, seeing his son had no intention of listening, moved to turn the broadcast off himself. Cal saw an opportunity to get close enough to the television to pick up a few words the woman was saying. He intercepted his father's hand before it reached the power button.

"It's not like I can't find out about it at school," Cal nearly growled. "Or in any corner of this dinky little town. Everyone wants to one-up each other with who's heard the latest details."

He strained to hear the woman on the screen, but she finished talking at the same time he did. The microphone held in front of her was pulled away, and Cal guessed that the field reporter was about to pose another question.

"Good. You can get your news there," Milo said, speaking over the reporter.

Cal seethed, but waited before replying so that the woman onscreen could answer. There was a chance he could piece together the question and what the story was about based on her response.

"*No, I had no idea,*" the woman's voice came through the TV just above a rasp. "*I was as surprised as anyone to see she'd fled in the middle of the night.*"

Milo saw what Cal was doing, and with his free hand cut the power to the TV. It didn't matter. Cal knew what the breaking news was all about. That hadn't been Sadie's father's deserted trailer, but Vin's mother's. Cal pieced together that being demonized around town for what her son had done had driven her to abandon the only home she'd known. Or perhaps it had become unbearable living in a home that reminded her of the monster she had raised.

Or perhaps she'd been overtaken by guilt from the knowledge that she had been the one who provided the evidence that linked her son to the crime.

Even though he'd gleaned the information he needed, Cal used *his* free hand to turn the television back on. Cal was undeterred by the look of incredulity Milo gave him. He'd gotten used to that look more and more over the last several years as he'd slowly tested the limits that he could challenge an authority he thought—no, *knew*!—was wrong. This was his boldest in a long history of defiance that had ramped up in the wake of discovering who'd killed Sadie Grimes.

"I'm not a child anymore," Cal snarled, hoping Milo would overlook how much he was behaving like one if he just insisted on it enough. "Stop trying to control me like you do with Mom. I've got a job. I'm saving up for my own ride. I—"

Cal stopped himself. He wasn't done lashing out at Milo, but he had the presence of mind not to clue in his hapless overlord that he slipped out of the house most Saturday nights when his parents had turned in for the night to go to parties, where he partook in a fair amount of drinking. Among other things.

"In a year and a half—no, *less!*—I'm outta here. Your role as my faithful watchman always trying to protect me will be over, so—"

"It's not *you* I'm trying to protect," Milo said, and even though Cal could tell he'd pushed his father to his breaking point, Milo's voice sounded more flustered than angry. "It's your—"

"Locket," a mousy voice squeaked behind them.

Both turned to see Cal's mother squinting through the puffy eyes of her bloated face at the television screen. They had become so caught up in their power struggle they hadn't heard her padded footsteps trudge down the carpeted hallway until she had joined them in the kitchen.

"That must've been why he went looking for her that day," she mumbled.

Cal gave her a peculiar look, then shot a quick glance at the screen. The woman and the abandoned mobile home had been replaced by the now infamous half-heart locket that Vin's mother had found tucked away in her son's old room with the rest of the belongings he'd never come back for.

The locket had been in fashion around the time Sadie had been presumed to have runaway, bought in pairs, with couples each keeping their half of the heart, usually placing the picture of their lover inside. Vin's mother had just been hoping to earn enough to cover her rent when she'd hawked it. There was no way to know that the police were looking for a locket with the inscription "SG heart VK Forever" because the police had never released that detail to the press when Sadie had first gone missing.

Cal honestly couldn't believe the man who ran the pawn shop even remembered that detail after all the time that'd passed.

His mother's face began to crumple. "Oh, Sadie," she cried. "Why'd you even have it?"

"Ruby," Milo said soothingly, taking a step toward his wife.

"You were so sure you had the baby," Ruby rasped, her voice dropping several octaves. She committed to entering the kitchen, expanding her distance from her husband as she made her way to the breadbasket. "But that night meant nothing to him. It . . . it was just what he did!" she wailed as she opened the basket, dug around, and found only bread.

"Ruby," Milo repeated, advancing step after cautious step.

Her head swiveled on her neck until she had captured the two of them in her suspicious sights. Cal made sure she caught him staring long and hard at his bookbag before returning her gaze. He was relieved to see her face sink. She was unlikely to tear the house apart looking for the vodka if she believed he'd taken it with him.

That wouldn't stop her from going out and buying another, though.

Cal didn't believe she'd openly accuse him of swiping her bottle. Exposing his theft would reveal that she had bought it in the first place, and if she wasn't worried about Milo knowing what she was washing her meds down with, she wouldn't have hidden the bottle in the first place.

"Ruby," Milo said as he closed the distance between him and his wife, "come with me. Let me help make it better like I did before," he said, putting a gentle hand on Ruby's shoulder as he tried to guide his wife back to their bedroom.

Cal had no idea what Milo was referring to, and assumed it'd been something that happened before he was born.

She shook his hand off. "It just made everything worse," Ruby gasped.

Her eyes widened, moving beyond her husband and landing on Cal, holding him with a look of embarrassment and regret, before they were cloaked in tears. "I'm sorry, my prince," she said before bursting into heavy sobs, dropping her eyes to the ground, finally allowing Milo to lead her out of the room.

Cal sneered at the back of the man who'd monopolized caring for Ruby. She may have submitted to her husband's will, but Cal despised Milo for his complete failure in curbing her daily regression.

"Yeah," Cal called down the hall at him, "you've been really successful helping Mom!"

He hated himself for smiling when his father stiffened. As expected, that was all Milo did before steering Ruby into the bedroom and closing the door behind them.

2: 1st Period

The student body was a-twitter over the morning's breaking news as they filed into school. Each pocket of conversation Cal picked up shared some new insight into the midnight escape. He wondered how much of it was conjecture, and how much was actual fact.

Cal didn't come across Zell until after homeroom, which was a shame. As he'd expected, Zell had plenty to share about Vin's mother, and Cal would've preferred scribbling his one-page essay during the ten-minute free period over trying to squeeze it in during the course of the day.

"Can't say I'm too surprised," Zell offered with a shrug. "She's been makin' noise about how intolerable th'harrassment's been for some time now." He gave another shrug, his usual mannerism for signifying he was about to make a counterpoint. "But, folks're lookin' for somewhere to vent their anger. And Vin isn't 'round t'face what he done."

Cal nodded, believing he had enough information to fill his required page. "Any idea where she might've gone?" he asked, seeing if he could add anything that would make his essay juicier. Anything Zell added wouldn't increase his grade. He either turned in a page, or he didn't. Cal just wanted to make his essay better if he could.

Zell's eyes looked skyward, zigging and zagging as if the answer to Cal's question was written on the ceiling, before he gave a shrug. "She'd have her pick among her kids. 'S'far's I know, th'rest of 'em still kept in touch with her after they moved out, but I doubt she's knockin' on any of their doors. They're as poor as her. Think she's got a sister in Michigan. That's where I'd go if I were her. If . . . you know, I had th'money."

"Right," Cal said with a nod, drafting his essay in his head. He knew that was the reason Ms. King hadn't skipped town the moment the police linked Sadie's death to her son. She was perpetually broke. He was about to ask where she could've come up with the cash when—

"*Calvin!*" a familiar voice cut through the crowd behind him.

The two of them turned to see Lance squirming his way through small slivers of the crowd. He was out of breath by the time he reached them.

"Did you run here from your house?" Zell asked with a smirk.

"I've been . . . calling your . . . name," Lance panted, ignoring the barb. "Didn't you . . . hear me?"

Cal shook his head. "Sorry, man. What's—"

"Do you know . . . if Cass . . . is in . . . today?" Lance wheezed, not waiting for Cal to finish.

"Haven't seen her," Cal replied, then offered, "She probably got a ride with Sherman." He didn't want to add that she'd been getting a ride to school from Sherman for the past month. He *did* feel like mentioning her insistence that she and Sherman were "absolutely *not* a couple."

"Okay," Lance said, still taking big gulps of air even after catching his breath. "Can you do me a favor? When you see her second period . . . can you remind her that . . . she needs to get a picture of . . . Morris Grimes this afternoon so we . . . have a photo of Sadie's father . . . for this month's newsletter?"

Cal took exception to the request. Cass wasn't one to forget her responsibilities, and took it personally when someone felt she needed reminding. He got the impression Lance didn't want his head chewed off, but still wanted the message delivered, and was trying to offer up Cal as a sacrificial lamb. The cowardice reminded him of his father, and perhaps not feeling he'd gotten his fill from the morning's fight, snapped at Lance.

"Why don't you tell her? You see her first period," he practically barked.

Lance shook his head. "Can't. I've got . . . ."

For a moment, Cal thought he was still short of breath. It wasn't until Lance continued, in a lower, softer voice, that it became clear what had caused Lance's voice to falter. "I've got an appointment with . . . ." His voice wavered again.

Zell jumped in and finished the thought for him. "Lafia."

The three of them stood there in silence amid the chatter of the town's murder. Further explanation was unnecessary. Cal's own appointment with Mr. Lafia was during fourth period tomorrow.

"I'll talk to her," Cal relented. "But in case I forget, you can always text her."

"Okay, thanks," Lance said, turning hesitantly toward the direction of Mr. Lafia's office, inhaling deeply in the desperate hope that he could suck up some courage, before departing as quickly as he'd materialized.

"I liked him better before he was weighed down by ambition," Zell remarked. "What's he so terrified for? I'd a'thought colleges'd be slittin' each other's throats t'recruit him. Isn't he takin' more advanced classes than you?"

Cal opened his mouth to reply but didn't know what to say. He'd already found from experience that it was difficult to explain the competitive nature of getting into an Ivy League university to someone who had no plans to enroll in college.

"Not everyone has their life mapped out already," Cal said, knowing that Zell planned on working full-time at his father's autobody shop after graduation. If Zell took the remark as a criticism for the lack of options he was leaving himself by forgoing college, he didn't show it, responding with his typical shrug and saying that he'd see him at lunch.

Cal just made it through the door before the first period bell sounded. He quickly found his seat before Mr. Pendergrass admonished him for his punctuality, but not so quick that he couldn't take note of what Polly was wearing. It came as a disappointment that she was not wearing a skirt again today, which drew a curse under his breath directed at the roller-coaster New England weather.

The desks were already arranged in a circle, allowing him another excellent view of her all day, if he wanted. Cal supposed it was beneficial that she wasn't wearing anything too distracting (her intoxicating beauty was already enough). There was still the short paper he had to write.

He pulled out his notes on yesterday's reading assignment, and placed it over a blank sheet of loose-leaf paper. His eyes then tracked Mr. Pendergrass as he paced around the room, a lion watching a gazelle until its back was turned before striking. Only he wouldn't lunge at his educator, he'd remove the top page and compose his essay, a handful of words at a time, covering his work with the top page again each time Pendergrass turned back in his direction.

To avoid suspicion, he raised his hand to the first few questions, and didn't begin working on his other assignment until he had answered twice. When he felt he'd planted the image of himself as engaged in the class discussion in Mr. Pendergrass' head, he went to work on his more pressing assignment, convinced that if the teacher saw him scribbling on a blank sheet of paper that it would be assumed he was taking copious notes.

For further motivation, he stole one last glance at Polly, and reminded himself that the faster he wrapped up his current events paper, the quicker he could get back to daydreaming about her. Tearing his eyes from her proved difficult. As his pupils drifted back to his paper, they caught a glimpse of other students watching Pendergrass intently before scribbling furiously. Cal smirked, seeing he wasn't the only one taking advantage of the way Pendergrass' classroom discussions allowed for the possibility to catch up on other assignments.

The irony was that Mr. Pendergrass had established this discussion format for his classes to ensure his students were engaged in the reading assignments. He hadn't changed his curriculum since Cal's parents had matriculated, and in that span, countless notes and analysis on all the classic works were easily referenced online, allowing pupils to forgo actually reading the books in lieu of skimming over a brief summation. Mr. Pendergrass had changed his approach to teaching, approaching the analysis of his beloved stories by posing questions examining why his favorite writers crafted their works the way they did, which usually took the form of "what if" statements.

"Who would like to tell me," Mr. Pendergrass began a new topic of discussion, "how they believe the climax would've played out if instead of being lashed at out of frustration over losing, the Bard had instead written the scene so that our hero was sliced with the poisoned blade during fair play?"

Cal suppressed his usual smirk. He relished how Mr. Pendergrass always referred to his absolute favorite playwright as the Bard, as though he was unworthy of uttering his name.

"Mr. Fisk?" Pendergrass inquired, and Cal tensed up, the name being so close to his own.

The boy called upon shrugged his shoulders. "What does it matter whether he was cut with the poisoned blade during the match or after? He got poisoned all the same, didn't he?"

Cal's hand shot up. He still had three quarters of a page to fill, but he'd felt he'd gone too long without participating in the conversation. A dose of paranoia was fine if it kept him cautious.

Pendergrass gestured for him to answer.

"There could have been massive repercussions. The hero might not have escalated the fight if he'd been bested fairly, which could've spared some lives, notably his opponent's. Revelations may not have come out in that final scene, and maybe the king would've gotten away with everything."

"Precisely," Mr. Pendergrass said, scratching at a haggard patch of his woolen sweater vest. It had taken Cal less than a month to determine Pendergrass had one for each day of the week. Being a Thursday, this one was green.

Satisfied that he'd contributed to the conversation, Cal returned to his essay.

"Anyone else?" Pendergrass asked.

Escaped further persecution, Cal scribbled.

"The queen."

Cal raised his eyes at the sound of Polly's voice.

"Seeing her son die from a mild cut may have tipped her off that the king had poisoned the sword as well. If she saw her son wasn't given a fair chance, she may have exposed the king's plot right then."

Cal flashed a smile that went unnoticed before returning to his paper. He supposed it was best if his infatuation with her remained a fantasy. Cass despised her and Cal didn't want to risk receiving the silent treatment.

Lightning rod of scorn, he scrawled, *for what many believed was decades of silence.*

"Excellent," Pendergrass remarked. "Anyone else?"

Speculation whether, he jotted, pausing to give a cursory glance at two of his classmates who were hotly debating whether the queen would've exposed that the king had poisoned the hero's cup as well. Cal focused his attention back on his essay . . . *she'd withheld more evidence from the investigation.*

"I'm not so sure any of this matters," Fisk exclaimed.

"Preposterous!" Pendergrass boomed.

Cal looked up to confirm Mr. Pendergrass was confronting Fisk before pouncing on his opportunity. Fisk sat practically opposite of him in the circle. Now that he had made his inflammatory remark, Pendergrass' back was to him.

"The sword was poisoned. The cup was poisoned," Fisk said in exasperation. "In all likelihood, the hero wasn't getting out of this. So, what difference does it make *how* he was poisoned?"

Cal couldn't believe his good fortune. He risked writing more words at once before sneaking a peek at Pendergrass.

Many believed she knew her son was still close to his victim.

"Mr. Fisk, the *way* in which the hero was poisoned makes *all* the difference," Pendergrass insisted.

Possession of the half-heart locket proved . . . he scribbled.

"Think of all the events that hinged on the king poisoning the blade as well as the cup. If the hero had merely been bested in the duel, or had drunk from the cup, and died, would you have found the ending satisfying?"

. . . Vin lied when he'd told the police he and the victim had grown apart, he scratched so furiously his words were barely legible.

Mr. Pendergrass coughed a chuckle. "It's the details, Mr. Fisk. Trust that the Bard knew what he was doing. It's these details that you find inconsequential that make the story, these minute decisions made by characters that carry the action. It's in these decisions that the Bard perfectly captured the way of life."

Ms. King had much to gain from her son avoiding incarceration.

A thokking sound accompanied his frenetic pace.

"Can anyone come up with an example of how one small decision impacted their own life?" Mr. Pendergrass threw out to the room.

The explanation Vin had given for his sudden enlistment had been to help his mother provide for his four younger siblings.

"My dad says the Sox would've won a championship if they hadn't drafted that Clark bum," Fisk offered, drawing giggles from the classroom.

Ms. King continued

"That's a fair example," Mr. Pendergrass conceded.

To receive benefits

"Mr. Fischer, could I see you after class?"

Cal's pencil froze against the paper. He was so mortified he didn't believe he'd ever cross the t he'd been working on. It was only when he stopped that he realized the heavy thokking sound had been coming from his own desk. Petrified, he lifted his eyes, which felt weighted down by anchors, to meet Pendergrass'.

"Can anyone think of anything else?" he asked, continuing on with the lecture as though he hadn't just caught Cal working on another assignment.

Polly raised her hand and waited to be called on. "I guess you could point to a whole number of things regarding the Sadie Grimes murder," she suggested. "Who knows how different things would've been if just one of the events leading up to her death had been different."

"An *excellent* point," Pendergrass chanted. "Indeed, while we may still not know everything that took place that night after a quarter century, plenty of details have surfaced, most of them gleaned in the past few months. What if Sadie *was* pregnant, as she and her father claimed. Surely that would've led the authorities to Vin King long ago. And if he were alive today, would he try to run? Would he risk going AWOL to avoid an arrest, knowing he would always have to evade the Army as well?" Pendergrass became overcome with the endless possibilities of what-ifs the crime offered. "Would he have ever been linked to the murder if Sadie hadn't paid to put that inscription on the half-heart locket?" Another thought popped into his head. "Think about where Randy Rogan would be right now if he hadn't won the contract to put up that shopping plaza. It would've been someone else who dug up poor Sadie's body in that meadow." There was no stopping him. "Someone else that finally gave closure to Morris Grimes. Someone else who lost everything when construction was suspended by the police investigation. Some—"

Mercifully the bell rang. The class let out a collective sigh. Cal didn't join them. He still had to speak with Mr. Pendergrass.

Cal ignored the ogles he got from his classmates as they lingered by the door, hoping to catch a glimpse of Mr. Pendergrass' admonishment.

"I'm sorry," Cal proffered.

He *was* sorry, too. Just not for writing the paper. He was sorry he'd gotten careless about keeping an eye on Pendergrass. If he hadn't, he doubted he'd be standing before him between classes.

"Usually senioritis doesn't take hold until a student is *actually* a senior," Mr. Pendergrass said, settling behind his desk.

Cal rolled his eyes. "I don't suffer from—"

"It's not *uncommon* to see cases crop up in some of the juniors," Pendergrass went on, uninterested in anything Cal had to offer. "But I've never seen one as advanced as yours."

This time, an eyeroll didn't seem sufficient. "I don't *have* senioritis," Cal snarled, as another student, Jamie, entered the room. The sophomore looked horrified at the tone Cal had taken with Pendergrass.

Cal ignored his audience. "Most classes I'm in are advanced something-or-other. My grades are excellent. If I *did* stop trying right now, I'd still coast to a B in this class." He knew that for a fact. He'd doublechecked. "I've got a job, and I still find the time to fit in—"

"I *know* you could coast to a B," Pendergrass cut him off, with a tone that suggested *he'd* doublechecked his gradebook as well. "That's my concern." He let out a deep sigh as he leaned back in his chair, vigorously clawing at the frayed patch of his vest, his fingers determined to burrow a hole through it. "Mr. Fischer, *had* you been giving today's discussion your full attention, you'd find it applicable to the conversation we're having now. Decisions, no matter how small, have ramifications on our lives. Yes, you've already passed my class with a few months still left in the school year. Yes, you'll score quite well, regardless of what you do the rest of the year. But is that the habit you want to set for yourself? Only doing the bare minimum to get by? Is that who you are?"

Cal felt himself wilting under Mr. Pendergrass' stare, even though he was standing over his teacher.

"Is that who you want to be?"

3: 4th Period

"Shut up!" Cass cried, laughing so hard she snorted. She put her hand over her mouth, contemplating spitting out the wad of her turkey sandwich.

Cass wasn't a stranger to talking with her mouth full, cramming her food to the side of her mouth with her tongue to speak, but she showed concern that she might choke to death guffawing over what Cal had just said.

"I'm serious," Cal said after washing down some crackers with a sip of water.

Cass managed to swallow her morsel of sandwich, but took another bite before continuing. "You've got Neil Fisk in your class, and Pendergrass hassles *you* about getting your act together?" she asked incredulously, before chortling all over again, and raising her hand to her mouth.

The napkin Zell offered her bobbed up and down to the beat of his own giggles.

Cal shook his head, suppressing a smile. "If he only knew how much energy I expend thinking that exact thing."

Cal finished the concluding statement on his paper and sighed. He knew he could have just waited until now to write his current events paper and avoided the lecture completely, but he'd chosen not to because working on his paper would've cut into the time he could enjoy with Cass.

The thought made his smile disintegrate. Cal assured himself they still saw each other a lot during the day. They even had one more class together this year than last. He still felt raw when she had snapped at him all the way back in October, and it still stung recalling she'd said she would "suffocate if we worked together, too."

She'd played it off like it would be beneficial if they both got different jobs because then they could enjoy each other's employee discounts. His wallet appreciated every dollar he saved toward a car, but he couldn't help see it as precious time he was losing with her. Cal had an inkling she felt the same way. Three waiters had quit in the past month, and she'd made sure to tell him there was an opening every time.

"Before I forget," Cass began, actually waiting to swallow her food before talking, "you're working on Saturday, right? Sherman wanted to see . . . oh, what was it again, some dumb superhero movie."

Cal did his best to hide his frown. He would've thought he'd mastered it with all the practice he'd gotten lately. "Is he picking you up? Bringing you chocolates? Flowers? Paying for dinner?"

"Oh, God," she said, with a roll of the eyes. "You guys don't let up. It's *not* a date!"

He wasn't sure why he felt relieved by the denial. But it *was* a denial. Her Saturday plans had centered around Sherman for the past five weeks. Not that he was counting.

"Yeah, I'll be working," he said, doing his best to keep the glum out of his voice. "Stop by, I'll hook you up with a jumbo popcorn you guys can share."

Cass shook her head as she finished off her sandwich. "No," her muffled voice weaved around the mashed bread in her mouth. "Sherman says eating popcorn upsets his stomach and gives him a headache."

Cal caught himself mid-eyeroll, grateful that Cass had glanced away momentarily. They'd already argued three times about Sherman, Cal passionately stating that she could do a lot better, and Cass maintaining they were not dating. Not that he was counting.

Zell had caught the eyeroll, and cast his friend a lifeline to spare him talking about a sore subject. "Speakin' of jobs, guess who I saw in th'hardware store yesterday?" he asked, already failing to suppress a grin.

"Oh, man, what'd my dad do now?" Cal asked.

Zell's giggling was contagious, and he hadn't even gotten to the punchline. "I didn't spot him 'til he was leavin'. He held th'door open for some old lady, but she must've been leadin' a parade, 'cause so many people walked in after her. And your dad held th'door open for *all* of 'em!"

This time Cass did spit her sandwich into her hand. Her head nearly collided with Cal's as they doubled over the lunchroom table in hysterics. Cal found it hard to gather himself, coming close twice, only to share a look with Cass that had them burst into a fresh wave of laughter.

"Oh, man," Cal said, wiping the tears from his eyes. "I wish I'd known *that* when Pendergrass was taking me to task. I would've had the *perfect* answer when he asked what sort of man I wanted to be. Because if I end up like my dad . . . well, you all have my permission to put me out of my misery."

"Your dad's not s'bad," Zell commented. "He really helped my dad with his bookkeepin' when he bought th'auto shop."

Cal fixed his friend with a sober frown. He knew Zell struggled to comprehend the vitriol Cal held toward Milo because Zell idolized his own father. Zell's father was proof you didn't need a 4.0 to be successful. It was apparent Zell welcomed his destiny to inherit his father's auto shop.

Truth be told, Cal had noticed an ever-increasing divide among his classmates between those who accepted the small-town life as the only path meant for them, and those who wanted to escape this pedestrian life by moving to the big city, *any* big city. The rift had become so obvious, Cal had noticed a key correlation among many of his classmates who showed no interest in ever leaving this podunk town. Most came from families who'd lived here for generations, and seeing that it had suited their parents, embraced the notion that this was where they were meant to be.

Cal's own parents were born and raised here. As were Cass and Lance's. The three considered themselves among a small coalition determined to pursue a lifestyle of their choosing, not dictated to them by factors like geography or demographics.

The first step in that pursuit was where they attended college, and none were as passionate about where they ended up as Cass. Cass detested her options, constantly bemoaning none of them were Julliard. The highest praise she gave any university was that she could at least save face if they accepted her.

Cal was about to respond when he felt sharp vibrations in his pocket. He frowned when he retrieved his phone. The call was from his mother. Whatever it was, it couldn't be good.

"Mom?" he answered as he left the table for some privacy. "Everything—?"

"—been obvious s'when all he'ever called'bout wasss the ssshopping center," Ruby was saying on the other end of the line.

Cal's frown sank so deep he thought his lips would droop below his chin. She'd probably been talking the moment she dialed his number, and likely didn't even notice the line had stopped ringing. His eyes glanced at one of the clocks hanging on the cafeteria wall. He concluded she'd found the bottle in the fridge. None of the liquor stores were open yet, which ruled out buying a new bottle. There *was* still the possibility she'd squirreled away others he hadn't found.

"Mom?"

"Never assked 'bout an'thing else 'rouund town," she said whimsically. "Only the ssshopping center."

Cass and Zell were giving him concerned looks. He moved away from the table. This was going to be a minute, and he didn't want them to hear how bad she was doing.

"Mom, you called. Is everything all right?" he asked a little louder, when he felt his voice would be drowned out from his friend's ears by the lunchroom chatter.

"The plans for the future," Ruby said in a serious, conspiratorial tone. "None o'vit includ'd ever coming back. Travel th'whirld! Tha's how it'us put. Ssso why'd'd h'care 'bout that . . . sshopping plasssa? And w—"

He couldn't make out the last part as a muted wail drew his attention, followed by "Answer me, you pencil-necked geek!"

Cal tilted his head to see that Jamie from Pendergrass' class, who'd been sitting alone, now had some companions at his lunch table. The sophomore's back was to him, but Cal didn't need to see his face to know the kid would've preferred to continue sitting alone. Milton Plunkett had sat down in one of the many empty seats, while his cronies stationed themselves around the table, watching the lunchroom monitors. One of them signaled to Milton, letting him know the monitor was distracted, and Milton landed a vicious Charley horse on Jamie's thigh. Jamie emitted that same pained wail.

Milton cocked his arm back, showing Jamie he was ready to deliver again.

"I've got your homeroom," Jamie replied, before his hands shot to cup his mouth. "*Homework*!" he corrected himself.

Milton lowered his fist slightly, waiting to confirm Jamie wasn't jerking him around.

Cal sighed. The kid was an easy target for the likes of Milton Plunkett. He knew Jamie a little from the debate team and the yearbook staff, enough to throw him a lifeline by inviting Jamie to his table so the sophomore didn't have to sit alone at lunch.

" . . . your father n'ver assked 'bout 'is mothher," Ruby continued to slur.

Cal turned his back on Jamie. His focus right now had to be his mother. Besides, he told himself, even if he rescued Jamic now, what good would that do him after next year, when he graduated, and Jamie was sitting by himself again, left to the mercies of Milton Plunkett.

"Is something wrong with Dad?" he asked.

His skin chilled when he was answered with a long pause. "Wanted t'know how th'biddin' was goin' on the sshopping plasssa," she rambled. "Always assked why they chose *that* spot t'build."

Cal's face sank. She'd entered the broken record phase of her stupor. Ruby could ramble like this for hours if he let her.

"Mom, I've got to go," he said, holding back a troubled tear from breaking loose.

"It was . . . how could I not *know*?" she pleaded, oblivious to anything he'd said.

"I'll make sure someone's with you tonight."

He refrained from ending the call with "I love you," while he was within earshot of Milton. He'd never met the savage personally, but jerks like Milton Plunkett had reputations that managed to get around before the first day of school ended.

"These better be right," Milton threatened Jamie.

Cal kept his back to them. He had more pressing matters to attend to. It sounded like the mayhem was over anyway.

Mom called, not doing well, can u watch her tonight? he texted.

He turned and stopped short when he saw Lance had joined his table. Cass glanced in his direction, sharing Cal's quizzical look.

"Jamie's a girl's name," he heard Milton taunt.

Cal didn't look until he heard a blistering slap.

His neck snapped to see Jamie seething, back rigid, shoulders flexed. Milton kept his open palm on Jamie's back where he'd smacked him. Cal imagined Jamie would be wearing a red handprint for days. Sensing he was being watched, Milton turned to meet Cal's gaze, his eyes challenging him to say something. Cal decided the prudent move was to keep walking. He didn't want any of what Milton was dishing out.

Even keeping his eyes forward, he could feel Jamie watching him, begging for salvation. It made walking by him painful, but not as painful as the red handprint had to be.

Cal didn't remember Lance looking so disheveled this morning. His friend had paled considerable since homeroom, and his glassy-eyed stare suggested he'd come from a battlefield instead of a morning of classes. Lance's appetite must've been insatiable at the rate he piled food into his mouth.

"Don't forget to breathe, buddy," Cal said, hoping a joke would snap him out of his trance. Lance's reply was to bite off half a granola bar before he'd swallowed the baby carrots he'd crammed into his mouth not five seconds prior.

"Hey, Lance," Cass said. "Don't you have lunch seventh period?"

That seemed to wake him from his stupor. He still scooped a gob of pudding into his mouth as he checked the closest clock. "Oh. Yeah. You're right."

"What's with you?" Cass asked, placing a reassuring hand on his forearm.

"Lafia."

Cal pulled up alongside him, and the three of them sat there silently, waiting for him to elaborate.

When he didn't, Zell asked, "Well, how bad was it?"

That drew a glare from Lance. "It was a bloodbath." For the first time since he'd sat down, he swallowed his food without immediately shoveling more into his gullet. "Betty Monroe's appointment with Lafia was right before mine. She came out of his office in tears. I knew I was in trouble then, but . . . I mean, I couldn't've ever imagined it would've been *that* bad."

"Well, what'd he say?" Cal asked, noticing for the first time that the table was shaking. When he looked down to investigate the source, he found it was his own trembling leg.

Lance shook his head. "It wasn't so much what he said, it . . . it was how quickly he honed in on things. When he asked what my plans were after I graduated, and I told him the colleges I was going to apply for, he opened my file, took one cursory glance, and immediately commented that I was lacking in extracurricular activities."

Cal winced. Lance had shared at least three times that he'd been having the same recurring nightmare, being barred from his top choices because he didn't participate in enough outside the classroom. He'd insisted he'd needed to devote all his focus to his workload this year. Lance would practically have a full semester of college credits under his belt before he ever stepped foot on any campus, double what Cal would have. Cal had warned him colleges looked at more than just grades, but knew now was not the time to bring it up.

"I opened my mouth to tell him that it was a calculated decision to ensure I scored well, but before I could get three words out, he finished my thought for me. Then he told me there're going to be thousands of other students applying to the same Ivy League schools who were going to get accepted over me because they'd spent the last year proving they could shoulder the demanding course load *and* find time to participate in the student body."

Lance glanced down absently at his pudding. He didn't seem to find the meal appetizing, but stuffed it into his mouth all the same. Cal got the impression his body was running on fumes after the session with Lafia, and would've eaten anything in front of him.

"You guys," Zell said with a chuckle, "place *way* too much emphasis on what Mr. Lafia says. You're actin' like it's guaranteed you won't get accepted t'any of your top choices because he said so. What happened t'the Lance who believed he controlled his destiny?"

"You don't *get* it," Lance growled rabidly. "The whole time I was in his office—" He stopped to reflect. "I don't think I could tell you the color of his eyes. He never even looked at me, just took one look at my transcripts and had me pegged. Knew everything I was going to say before I said it. It was like he'd been doing this for so long, nothing I said or did could surprise him. Like he'd seen me in countless other students of years past, could recollect how life had played out for them, and knew the same fate awaited me."

His head sank, and Cal knew that as bad as it had been, Lance still hadn't revealed the worst.

"The advice he ended with was to reconsider which colleges I was applying for if I already felt I couldn't keep up with what others were accomplishing."

Cal clapped his friend on the back, while Cass squeezed his forearm. Lance didn't respond to either comfort.

"So maybe you don't get into th'most prestigious school, so what?" Zell shrugged.

Lance grew ill-tempered. The only thing that kept him from casting Zell in his malice-filled gaze was that he didn't want to risk the others seeing how close he was to tears.

"Some of us didn't want to settle for the hand life dealt us," Lance rasped.

Cal didn't think he was being fair to Zell, but wasn't sure he could reach his friend in this fragile state. He'd never seen Lance this close to erupting, and wasn't sure Lance even knew what emotions would pour out if the dam burst.

The buzz from his phone allowed him to avoid the issue. He rolled his eyes even before he read the text.

Sorry, you know it's my busy season.

He didn't know what he'd expected when he sent his message. A memory surfaced, demanding his attention. He vividly recalled the enthusiasm Ruby had expressed the one time she'd tried to convince Milo to not only take a vacation, but take them somewhere. She'd done her best to hide it, but Cal was old enough to recognize the disappointment in her eyes, just like he'd been old enough to see something in Milo's. For years, Milo had given excuses why he never interviewed for a new job ("My commute is perfect!"), tried new foods ("My stomach's sensitive") or traveled ("My job needs me, I'm close to becoming the manager"). It wasn't until that moment Cal understood Milo wasn't just set in his ways, he was scared of change, and allowed that fear to dictate every decision in his life. That was the moment Cal knew life wasn't meant to be lived in fear. That was also the moment Cal decided he was going to live life his way.

He shoved the phone back into his pocket, then studied his friend in silence. Maybe his own session with Mr. Lafia wouldn't go so poorly. Maybe he wouldn't come out of it devoid of all hope.

Cal had to believe that. Had to believe his life could be whatever he made of it.

He just couldn't accept that all his efforts over the last couple of years were futile in the face of turning into someone who couldn't help his mother.

4: 7th Period

Cass passed him the note with impunity. Cal accepted it without a cursory glance at Mrs. McCauley. As long as the class kept the noise down, she'd keep her eyes glued to the television. The students in her classes had learned early on that talking wasn't permissible because it interfered with the broadcast, but passing notes, if the ruffling of folded paper was kept to a minimum, was acceptable.

He read the message quickly, then turned and shook his head. She mouthed "Work?" then gave a sharp look when Cal opened his mouth. Cal turned to see the program was just coming back from a commercial and, deciding not to risk Mrs. McCauley's ire, jotted down his explanation and handed the note back to her.

The round of applause from the studio audience was just starting to die down. Mrs. McCauley was really testing the limits of her tenure today. Usually, she had restricted the viewings to the local news, but because the scheduled guest was going to be covering such a juicy topic, she decided a talk show now fit the parameters of education.

When Cal turned back to Cass to gauge her reaction, he considered the disappointment in her eyes promising. She had wanted him to come over after school. He pushed down the notion that with him unavailable she'd turn to Sherman next, or that the reason she looked so glum now was that Sherman had already turned down the invitation.

"*We're joined now by Jane Chaplin,*" the talk show host was saying. "*Thank you for coming.*"

Cal felt a tapping on his shoulder, and turned to see Cass handing him another note. In the front of the room, Mrs. McCauley took no notice, her full attention devoted to the interviewee graciously accepting being there.

He stopped working on his physics assignment to read the message. After drawing a frowning face, Cass had asked if his mother was really doing that bad.

"*Now, at the top of the show, when I told the audience we were going to be meeting someone who* dated *Vin King, you could hear a pin drop,*" the host was saying. "*Can you tell us what it was like being in a relationship with a murderer?*"

The woman being interviewed took a moment to inhale deeply. Her eyes were already welling up with tears. Cal laid the note down on his physics homework, knowing both would be abandoned until the class ended.

Ever since the town's greatest mystery had finally been solved, history with Mrs. McCauley had turned into his favorite class. Mrs. McCauley, as hungry for new details as everyone else, had advocated for a television in her classroom, arguing that there was no point in teaching history if she ignored it when it was happening right in front of them.

"*You have to understand,*" Jane began. "*I'm just one of a long line of girls.*" That drew gasps from the studio audience. "*He was a real charmer back then.*"

The most advanced history class the high school offered became the easiest. Each day, Mrs. McCauley only taught for half the period, before turning on the TV, finding an empty seat in the front row, and watching the nonstop coverage of the Sadie Grimes murder with her students.

"*He had a way of making you feel special,*" Jane reflected. Her melancholy tone suggested she might have regretted that it didn't work out. "*He had these grand plans for what he'd do after he graduated, and whenever he got going on the subject, he'd always include me, as if all his future happiness hinged on me being there to share in those moments with him. And then there was our 'special place' where he took me for a picnic. But when I saw the footage of the cops digging up the meadow where the shopping center was supposed to go, I realized I wasn't the only girl he'd taken there.*"

The course load remained as rigorous as ever, even more so now that the time spent reviewing the subject matter had been slashed in half. But with a half period of "free time," Mrs. McCauley's students never floundered in keeping up with their assignments. Cal had researched and drafted most of his Civil War paper from his seat in this very classroom.

The glorified study hall provided an opportunity to catch up on his other assignments, as well. Cal had Spanish next period, but tended to wait until this class to fill out his worksheets. More than once he'd used the last half of his history class to draw up flashcards for an upcoming test. The only times he felt in danger of not completing an assignment came when the news anchors had breaking news to report, which they typically withheld until the evening broadcast.

"It didn't bother you back then knowing he'd dated all those other girls?" the talk show host inquired.

Cal knew today was going to be one of those classes he didn't get a head start on his schoolwork. It was both inconceivable how far Mrs. McCauley was pushing the limits of learning by watching television (Cal and Cass joked "Look! It's our teachers" each time they passed a billboard of the news team), yet captivating to listen to a woman who knew Vin King intimately.

Jane Chaplin shook her head, her face growing red from the strain of trying to keep her tears in check. *"I was just a silly little girl back then. We all were. I remember I was so enamored with his slick hair. And his eyes. I loved the way he'd look at me. And, I know this sounds foolish, but I just loved his chin."*

There was an eruption of chortles a few rows behind him. Mrs. McCauley twisted her neck around, her eyes muting the ruckus disrupting her afternoon viewing habits. Cal cast an angry glance over his shoulder. They were jeopardizing a good thing. The last thing he wanted was to hear a lecture on history for a full class. He wasn't sure he was conditioned for it anymore.

Cal half expected Cass to be awaiting a response to her note. Her attention was focused solely on the interview.

"*Would you*"—the host began, then paused for dramatic effect—"still *feel that way about Vin King? If he was still here, I mean?*"

Jane's face caved in on itself. It was no use trying to hold back the tears now. The host handed her a freshly opened box of tissues. Cal was sure the show's producers were eating it up. He could imagine that exchange had been used in all the promos for today's show.

"*No. What I had with Vin, what* most *of us had with Vin, was just a fling. He had a way of seducing you, but we all learned that as rapidly as he got you into bed, he got bored with you even faster.*" She sobbed gently into an already soaked tissue. "*That was when I learned how little I meant to him.*"

"*Did* all *his exes feel that way?*" the host pried.

Another long pause. Another shake of the head.

"*Not Sadie.*"

A hush fell over the classroom at the mention of the name. If conversation in the back of the room was still going on, it halted immediately. Notes being passed, doodles being sketched, phones being played with, everything came to a standstill, and everyone leaned in to hear what she was going to say.

"*She must've been crazy about him,*" Jane said. She had surrendered in the fight to hold back tears, weeping openly now. "*He used her as a means to dump us. The coward couldn't tell us directly that he was over us. Instead, he'd just stop calling, stop returning our calls and wait for us to hear the rumors that he'd been seen around town with Sadie again. He'd flaunt the affair until we couldn't ignore it anymore and understood the relationship was over.*" She shrugged. "*Then he'd discard Sadie again while he looked for a new conquest.*"

The entire classroom watched with rapt attention. In the months of round-the-clock coverage since the story had broken, it was incredible to think there were still new details emerging that had led to the Grimes' girl's death.

Cal, as he always did when new information surfaced, held onto every word, trying to place himself in the shoes of someone who'd experienced this mystery from the beginning. What he knew of Vin King stemmed from news reports a quarter century after the crime had been committed. The only testimonies he'd heard from people who knew the rogue were Vin's mother and Sadie's father, and both were clearly biased. This interview was unique. The woman held no agenda. The relationship was long over, the lover long gone. The free-flowing tears told Cal the woman was still shaken over having let herself get so close to a killer. The only thing she had to gain from sharing her story was closure.

Try as he might, he couldn't comprehend why girls had continued to line up for dates with Vin. Good looks could only go so far. The biggest enigma of the lot was why Sadie allowed herself to be used so publicly. In the *many* interviews that Morris had given over the years, he lambasted the town labeling his daughter as troubled, while she was alive, missing, and later, found dead. Cal peeked over his shoulder at Cass, curious if she might be able to provide some insight into what Vin's appeal could have been.

"*If he had someone always waiting for him with open arms, why do you think he killed her?*" the host asked.

Cass's cheeks reddened when she caught him staring at her. His own seemed to heat up, which was odd. They'd never had these awkward exchanges last year. She quickly pointed to the note on his desk.

"*I think because she became as clingy as the rest of us,*" Jane replied, before letting out another deep sigh. "*They were seniors when she 'went missing.' We were all going our separate ways. I don't think he was planning on enlisting yet, but he wasn't sticking around town after he graduated, either. Looking back on it now . . . I think she was okay with letting him stray because he was always close by, and it was easy to come back to her. But if he left . . . well . . . things might really be over.*"

Cal began jotting that his mother was getting worse because of course Milo didn't know how to make her better.

"I didn't know her well enough to know if she'd lied to her father about the pregnancy," Jane went on. Her head sank until it was practically resting in her bosom. Her face was filled with shame, and Cal was convinced she was among the many that had called Sadie a slut at one time or another. *"For years, I thought maybe her father was lying about her being pregnant. Every time he was being interviewed, I wanted to storm out of the room, or throw something at the television. It wasn't until I thought about the source of my scorn for Morris Grimes that I realized it stemmed from what Vin had told me about him, that he was just a drunk who'd tell any lie it took to change people's mind about him and his daughter."*

Cal stopped writing to devote his attention to the television again. He didn't think Jane had been too far off in her initial assessment of Morris.

The room groaned as Principal Utzig's voice announced over the PA system that tonight's drama class was cancelled, as it drowned out the next question the host posed.

Cal leaned forward in his desk until it began to tip over.

"No, I don't think being a father was what made him kill her. I think it was her being the mother. He was seeing a girl at the time. Their relationship looked like it was on the same trajectory ours had been. All the signs were there. Vin and Sadie were inseparable. But this time, when he tossed Sadie by the wayside, he was still with the girlfriend. Sadie being pregnant might've jeopardized that. So was getting the half-heart

locket. As soon as I heard Vin's mother had pawned the locket with that inscription, I knew what'd happened: Sadie had swiped the locket his current girlfriend had given him when Vin had been using Sadie to break up with her. Sadie possessing the locket was how she'd blackmailed Vin to meet her to tell him she was pregnant." Jane shook her head. "*I remember being envious of that girlfriend. There were nights I screamed into my pillow 'What does she have that made her a keeper?'*"

"*You wished he'd chosen you back then?*" the host probed.

For the longest time, all Jane could manage were nods.

The bell rang, bringing a chorus of moans. It felt like the interview was just reaching its apex, but they all had to leave. Cal focused his ears amid the packing up and shuffling feet. His efforts looked destined to go unrewarded; Jane remained mute. Even Mrs. McCauley had abandoned hope, reaching for the dial to turn it off. She stayed her hand when Jane forced herself to continue.

"*Yes,*" she confessed, streams of tears pouring down her face. "*Even after what he did to us, none of us expected him capable of that. We were just . . . drawn . . . to his magnetism. Despite what he'd done, I wanted a second chance. I almost told him I could be his Sadie. Several times. But*—thank God— *I kept getting cold feet. I . . . I . . . .*"

Mrs. McCauley's hand was shaking as it hovered over the dial. Cal urged her not to turn it off, not now.

To think, the fates of two women had been decided by which one was willing to subject themselves to Vin's selfish appetites.

Jane paused to collect herself, swallowing hard. *"Sometimes I wake up screaming, thinking about how that could've been me buried in that meadow."*

5: Yearbook Club

"I don't disagree," Polly replied, and Cal had to hold back a smile. The way her nose crinkled when she tried to keep the annoyance in check was adorable. "But at some point, we're going to have to draw the line on what gets included about the murder."

"Okay," Patel, another junior on the yearbook staff, continued to argue, "but this *definitely* needs to—"

"The printer already gave us a hard deadline of the sixth of May if we want to be able to distribute copies before the year lets out," Polly insisted, casting another furtive glance at Lance, who was still flipping through pages of an academic programs booklet, lost in his own world.

"Which means we've still got a couple weeks to create the outline," Cathy, a sophomore who was as passionate about getting her ideas as everyone else in the room, stated.

Polly's eyes widened as she took a moment to keep her temper from exploding. Cal sensed she had expected this meeting would go smoothly without Cass there to bicker with. What made it more challenging was that the club's leader had engrossed himself in the task of searching for extracurricular activities to pad his college applications.

"Is that what you want, though?" Polly politely challenged the group. "To turn in some rush job to the printer because we wanted to include some new rumor we heard? Wouldn't we all rather spend these last weeks polishing our layout so it looks spectacular?"

Cal opened his mouth to say it was an excellent point, feeling uninhibited because Cass was across town getting a snapshot of Morris for the school paper, when Mandy Ryan said, "Cal, you brought up Vin's former lover. Don't you think we should try to include a picture of her?"

Mandy wasn't the only one who hadn't been swayed by Polly's reasoning. Three heads were bobbing up and down.

"That wasn't the reason I brought it up," Cal answered, turning back to Lance.

His friend had turned his attention from the programs booklet to the newspaper splayed on the table in front of him. Both had been butchered in red ink, with jobs and clubs circled and then crossed out, tornados drawn over listings that didn't bear consideration, and random marks where Lance had jabbed at the pages when the process had grown overwhelmingly agitating.

Cal had brought up Jane Chaplin's story at the club, hoping it would snap Lance out of his funk. If a woman could potentially save her own life deciding not to pursue the affections of a sociopath, surely Lance had some say over where he went to college.

"Lance," Polly said, exhaling deeply through flared nostrils. She'd grown weary of all the decisions falling squarely on her shoulders. "Do *you* think we should still be adding to the design?"

Cal knew she was banking on Lance to dismiss the latest alteration as swiftly as he'd rejected Cal's theory that Jane's survival derived from her own choices. After Cal had presented the story, Lance speculated that Lafia probably still kept records on every student who'd matriculated here, and that Jane Chaplin's file would state her personality wouldn't tolerate the selective affections of Vin King the way Sadie's had. That being the case, Jane was never at risk because Sadie's level of acquiescence wasn't in her nature.

"Hmm?" was all Lance offered, before drawing an X through another job listing he'd circled and emitted an exasperated sigh as he surveyed the periodicals before him. His eyes were nothing more than bleak-looking glasses as he scanned the pages again in the hopes he'd made a mistake in his previous readthroughs. He shook his head at running for student council, the elections having been held two weeks ago. Shook his head at prom committee, as they met the same time this club did. Drama club drew another shake of the head for the same reason. Chess club, another shake. He applied a fresh coat of red ink to all the team sports.

Polly reluctantly accepted she'd have to continue leading the meeting. "We shouldn't even *consider* including coverage of more alumni from twenty-five years ago if we can't even obtain the yearbook photos of Vin and Sadie from the year they graduated."

During the first yearbook meeting held after the half-heart locket had surfaced, the club had unanimously voted to change the theme from the generic "One Chapter Closes, A Brighter One Lies Ahead" to coverage of a town finally reaching closure on the most horrific chapter of its history. The school faculty admonished them for even considering turning the theme into such a morbid topic, but Principal Utzig eventually relented when several of the yearbook staff stated their parents had told them the Grimes' girl's disappearance had been the theme of the yearbook when *they'd* attended this high school.

While Mr. Utzig had reluctantly permitted them to proceed, he and the rest of the faculty offered no cooperation. The only edition of the school's yearbook not available in the library was the one publication they were trying to emulate. At first, it was regarded as nothing more than a petty roadblock. It wasn't until their parents told them that although they vividly remembered the salacious theme, they had no idea where their old yearbooks were, or if they even still had them, that they understood the height of the mountain they were attempting to scale.

"Ahem," a squeaky voice interrupted.

The whole table, even Lance, turned to a shy freshman holding an old yearbook. Like Cal, most couldn't remember hearing her voice before.

"Cynthia Morrison! You're my hero!" Mandy exclaimed.

Cal joined the stampede of students leaping from their seats to huddle around Cynthia.

"My dad found it while he was cleaning out our garage yesterday," Cynthia explained. "Sorry the front cover is scuffed. It was under his bowling trophies."

"It's fine," Mandy insisted as she took the lead in flipping the pages of the elusive yearbook.

"Look, they were calling it a disappearance back then," Patel noted.

"Makes sense," Polly observed. Cal stiffened at her voice, aware for the first time he was standing right next to her. "Her body wouldn't be found for another four years."

She bent forward to get a closer look, and the side of her hip touched the back of Cal's pinky. A burst of electricity surged through Cal, ecstatic to be *touching* her! And not just a grazing touch. She was leaning against him. He glanced around the room, seeking a confidant to share in this moment, and frowned when he saw Lance was still seated, still searching for something to salvage his application.

The rest of the club took no notice of Lance's manic state. They flipped through the pages, breathing a collective sigh of relief that the theme they were running with this year wasn't a carbon copy of what their parents had done. Where the yearbook that Cynthia had brought in captured a tone of shock and the efforts to return to normalcy (because these things didn't happen in nice little towns like theirs), the current yearbook had adopted a tone of closure.

The flipping of pages continued until they reached the G's in the senior class. Sadie's photo stuck out on the page, partly because it'd been the go-to image by all the local news stations, and partly because she'd been the only one not wearing a black dress. Cal recalled his grandmother had still been complaining last year about the cost of his mother's senior picture dress.

The yearbook had gained Ouija board properties. A collection of hands continued turning the pages.

"There he is!" Mandy rasped.

It was the same image they'd seen countless times. Yet there was something about seeing it on the page that made *this* viewing significant.

"He looks like every other boy," Cynthia noted.

"Anytime someone commits a heinous act, everyone says the same thing," Polly said, standing up straight again. She gave Cal a quick glance that looked dismissive. "He was always such a nice boy."

"Look at this," Patel said, still perusing the yearbook.

Cal's heart beat in his throat at the new picture of Vin. Although he'd never seen a picture of her at that age, the girl smiling alongside him was unmistakably his mother.

There was a banner above the two of them that read "Homecoming." She was in uniform, her hands swallowed by two giant poms. They were standing on the corner of the bleachers in the school's gymnasium, the rest of the school body roaring their approval at something taking place out of the frame.

He massaged his chest, relaxing himself. It was just a pep rally. The school photographer had needed some coverage for the event, and Vin and his mother just happened to be close by. The image had only shaved a year off his life because of who Vin turned out to be.

"Let's just stick with their class pictures," Cal suggested. "No sense linking more people to the senseless murder."

"Good idea," Polly said, and Cal was positive he'd seen the faint trace of a smile. She turned to the group. "Does anyone besides Cass have a copy of our layout?"

"Chuck does, but . . . ." Mandy started to reply. The club looked around the room, aware for the first time Cass wasn't the only one missing.

"But what?"

"I haven't seen him since his meeting with Mr. Lafia," Mandy answered glumly.

"When was that?" Polly asked, concern finally present in her voice.

"Fifth period. Yesterday."

"I habit," Jamie croaked, before his hands shot to his mouth and he flushed with embarrassment. "*Have it,*" he corrected himself, pushing away from the table and stooping over a bookbag busting at the seams.

Cal had passed by Jamie's locker on his way to the meeting, and had noticed Jamie's valiant efforts zipping the pouches closed. When he'd arrived at the meeting, Jamie had nearly toppled over slinging the bag off his shoulders, and the club had teased him that the tile floors were likely to crack under its weight. Cal couldn't recall a time he'd needed to bring home all his textbooks in his sophomore year, but had forgotten about the oddity until now.

"Great," Polly said. "I'll make a copy of Vin and Sadie's class pictures, we'll add them to the layout, and *if* we still have space, we'll use a picture of this Chaplin woman."

The club was all smiles the rest of the meeting. Except for Lance, so absorbed he didn't even notice when they'd adjourned, even with Jamie struggling to hoist his bag onto his back.

"Want me to see if the school's got a cot you can sleep on?" Cal ribbed gently.

It was concerning when Lance didn't snap a comeback at him, or at the very least tell him to fuck off. Instead, Lance just buried his head in his hands, not sobbing, just sitting there quietly.

Cal thought his friend was content to keep that pose forever when he finally blurted out "It's hopeless."

"Oh, stop sulking," Cal scolded him.

"It's *hopeless!*" Lance snarled, pounding his fists on the table. His wild red eyes held Cal. "I've been combing through these all day," he stated, lifting the assortment of pages in front of him and letting them plop back on the table. "There's nothing I can take on to improve my standing in the eyes of admission boards. Nothing! The part-time jobs this town has to offer are pathetic. Any of the clubs I'd be interested in somehow manage to be held at the same times of the clubs I'm *already* in. I'm too uncoordinated to join any teams. The volunteer work is on the other side of town, and with no job, I can't afford to get there."

Lance stared for miles at nothing in particular. "You were right," he said softly, referencing the advice Cal had given him every time Lance had one of his nightmares.

"You just need a good night's sleep," Cal said as he rounded the table and coaxed his friend to get up. "Remember, you've only been at this a few hours."

Lance stiffened in his arms. "I've been at this my whole life." He turned to Cal, tears welling up as much as they could without crying. "Do you have any idea, the grueling toll it takes on you, chasing a dream everyone tells you to abandon, day after day, year after year, only to come to the end and find they were right all along?"

6: Evening

Cal placed a hand over the receiver of his phone as he tiptoed out of the living room. Neither action seemed to matter. Mr. Banks was too absorbed in his lecture to hear Ruby's ramblings in the background, and Ruby was too sloshed to notice much of anything.

"*I've got a business to run,*" Mr. Banks said on the other end of the line. "*Tonight's the start of the weekend rush.*"

"I know, Mr. Banks, I'm sorry," Cal said. "It's just"—he cast a glance at Ruby, still mumbling to herself as she stared vacantly at the television—"I'm still dealing with a personal matter."

"Whenn'uzz *my* trial? Hmm? I don' r'membrer g'ttin' one," Ruby decried from the other room.

"*Cal, you've been calling in for two weeks,*" Mr. Banks stated. "*It's not fair having everyone else cover your shifts.*"

"I'll be in tomorrow," Cal insisted. "And, I've already talked to Devin about covering his on Saturday." He hadn't, but Devin always bemoaned how working Saturdays kept him from taking Courtney (maybe it was Caroline) out on dates. Now that the weather was starting to warm up, Devin was sure to jump at the chance to take her out.

"Wha' wuzz *my* crime?" Ruby wailed.

Mr. Banks sighed. "*I'll give you one last chance, Cal. Only because you're a good kid. But if you throw this back in my face—*"

"I won't, Mr. Banks," Cal said hurriedly. "Thank you, Mr. Banks." He hung up before his boss had time to reconsider.

"My prince! Wher'd'you go?" Ruby bellowed from the living room.

"Here, Mom," he said, returning to the room and taking his spot on the couch within arm's reach of her.

The hours were insufferable. He slogged through his assignments, unable to focus amids her endless ramblings. She entered her broken record mode, and Cal caught himself tallying the number of times she asked what her crime had been in the margins of his notebook. Cal didn't have to review his work to know they were plagued with wrong answers and spelling errors. He gave up working on his assignments when he saw he'd written "What was my crime?" as an answer to one of his math problems. There was no point redoing any of it tonight. His mother showed no signs of slowing down, and he'd only grow more frustrated and make more mistakes if he started over.

He left the room twice and he regretted it both times. The first time had been to use the bathroom. When he came back, he found her pouring more of a freshly opened bottle of wine on the couch than in her glass. This one had been tucked behind their Blu-rays, the cabinet door left wide open. He snatched the bottle from her as he searched for something to soak up the spill.

"I jus' donno why'm bein' punissht," Ruby pouted when he returned with wads of paper towels. "Whaddid I'do?"

He ignored her as he padded the damp areas. Her transition to whites at least had its benefits, and for the same reason. The stains left on her teeth had betrayed her drinking in the early days. Cal studied the couch after he was done cleaning up. In time it would dry, the smell would dissipate, and there would be no evidence of her daily binging.

The second time he'd left had been to make them dinner. When he came back this time, she had changed the channel to one of the news stations. It was the first time she'd paid any attention to the programs all night.

Morris Grimes sat behind a desk, hunched over a microphone held in front of him. Cal couldn't tell for sure, but it looked like the field reporter interviewing him was gently tugging it from his grasp.

"*Which is why I'm selflessly founding The Sadie Grimes Foundation,*" he said, grandstanding into the mic.

Morris paused, posing for the shutterbugs of the media at his now daily press conferences. Cal wondered if Cass was among them as he swooped in and changed the channel.

He'd heard enough about the foundation, an organization Morris had prattled on about, starting going all the way back to when Sadie's body had first been unearthed. It was going to provide counseling for girls who were depressed, provide college grants, establish fundraisers to help the less fortunate, even supply housing for women needing to escape abusive relationships. For all the grand plans Morris promised from the foundation, it sounded no closer to launching since he'd announced it.

Ruby's hand shot to the dial, flipping it back to Morris. "*Not everyone is capable of withstanding the slander I had to hear about my Sadie, and* myself, *and I won't rest until I'm assured no one else endures what*—"

Cal changed the station again. "C'mon, Mom. It's no good listening to that."

Ruby's head bobbed up and down, weeping silently to herself. "Why'm I all wayss punisssht?" she begged.

Cal grew disconcerted with the way her words were leaning on one another. It was an indication they were in for another rough night.

"Who'd *I* hurt? H'said h'was okay withhit. Milo said h'diddint mind."

She repeated that for the next hour, even after Milo walked through the door, exhausted. Milo took one look at his son, saw Cal was ready to snap all his pencils in two, then one look at Ruby, swaying but not quite toppling over, and emitted a deep sigh, accepting his night wouldn't get any easier.

"You diddint mind," Ruby greeted him.

"I thought you had work," Milo said to Cal.

Cal rolled his eyes, gesturing at his mother. "She can't be left alone, can she?"

Milo sat his briefcase by the door, along with three accordion folders, a new record for this year. "Sorry, Cal," he said, rubbing his temples as he made his way toward the kitchen to brew himself his nightly pot of coffee. "Roger needed me to stay late so he could take—"

Cal scoffed, rolling his eyes so irately he thought they'd fly out of his sockets. "What're you taking orders from a guy who's only been there five years?"

"I know I told you he's—" Milo said, startling Cal when his voice boomed, before cutting himself off, acting as though he wouldn't take Cal's bait.

Cal found the air suffocating. He needed to escape. There was no doubt this nightmare homelife scenario was exacerbated by his father's fear of change. Cal was convinced Milo's bosses kept riding him because they knew Milo was afraid to lose the one job he'd ever had, despite what little regard they showed him. Rather than tell them to shove it, Milo accepted his grueling schedule that kept him from home, even if it meant failing his family, especially his wife, who needed support now more than ever.

And whenever he *was* home, despite insisting it was his responsibility, he was often too exhausted to care for Ruby. Cal shook his head, thinking it should have been Milo ordering Roger to stay late so he could take care of things. Cal doubted Roger was dealing with the level of turmoil they were.

While he listened to Milo rummaging through the kitchen, he sent a text asking if it was too late to accept the invitation. Cal smiled at the promptness of the response.

Sure! My parents won't mind. June's visiting.

Cal slipped into his shoes as he stalked toward the kitchen. The familiar jingling settled on the countertop, but Cal waited until Milo's footsteps trudged toward the cupboards before he pounced.

"Hey!" Milo exclaimed when he caught Cal snatching his keys. "It's a school night!"

"So were the last two times I slipped out," Cal shouted, astonished with the brashness of his own confession. Cal had felt he could've graduated before Milo ever caught wise to his late-night adventures.

"Therwuzz no victim!" Ruby hollered from the living room, before softly adding, "Only me."

They both turned to the sound of her voice. "I need help with your mother," Milo said, gently, almost pleading.

The groveling disgusted Cal. "Is that the burden you'd place on your own son? I was here all night for her. Where were you? Oh, that's right. Staying late. *Again*! Because Roger made you."

Cal stormed for the door. He would've let it go at that, until he heard Milo pipe up. "I know this can't be easy for you, seeing your mother in this state. Maybe it *would* be best if you took a break from this. I suppose it'd be healthy to get a little mental reset from this chaos. Just this once."

He fumed, clenching the brass doorknob, unable to contain the powder keg rumbling within. The man was actually attempting to frame Cal's exit as an allowance he was granting.

"Who are you trying to fool?" Cal roared. "Because it ain't me! I don't need your permission for *anything*. I'm in control of my actions. *Me*!"

"Cal, why are you acting this way?"

That earned a laugh. "Because I *choose* to! You disapprove? Good! It means my efforts not to end up like my worthless father are working." The frown his words drew broke his heart, but in his angst he felt compelled to twist the knife further. "The last thing I want to become is the guy who lost out on the promotion he'd been groomed for because some jerkoff named Roger showed management *he* wasn't a pushover."

7: Cass's

The laughter coming up through the floorboards calmed him. Merriment within a family residence seemed alien when Cal compared it to the havoc taking place in his own home. He pressed his ear against the faded tan carpeting of Cass's room to hear the muffled happiness better.

"You're really not worried?" Cass asked from her bed, scratching away in one of her many notebooks.

"What's my dad going to do?" he asked, failing to keep the hostility out of his voice. "Even if he tried to ground me, he knows he can't make it stick. He's got his hands full with work and Mom. He's got no time to keep an eye on me. Besides, I'll have my *own* car soon, and not long after that, this town is going to be in my rearview mirror."

The rampant scrawling in her notepad came to a stop, and Cal braced himself. Cass had a knack for writing while conversing and not losing her train of thought on either, only stopping the former if she had to share bad news via the latter.

Right on cue, the hesitant pause prefaced her next statement. "Speaking of which, I've decided," she began, before taking another cautious breath. This was going to be a doozy. "I've decided to apply for Dartmouth."

She flinched when he snapped his head her way. "We agreed!"

"I know," she said, repentant.

"We were putting distance between ourselves and this town. That meant nothing in state."

"I *know*," she said, defensively.

"We were making a statement we could survive out from under our parent's shadows."

"*I know!*" she said, hotly.

Before he could press on, the door swung open. Cass's mother barged in, angry eyes focused on her daughter.

"*Cassiopeia!*" she hissed venomously. "When someone's in the room with you, the door stays *open!*" she reiterated what must have been a household rule. Her mother spared them all embarrassment not emphasizing this only applied to boys.

"We're just *friends!*" Cass blared back at her mother.

Cal joined in, though with much less passion.

Cass's mother softened her gaze when she regarded him lounging in his usual spot on the floor. "How's your mother doing?" she asked with a frown.

Something flickered in her eye, leaving Cal to wonder if his mother's condition wasn't such a secret after all. She had to leave the house to get to the liquor store. This was a small town. Which loved to talk. And even with the murder, there wasn't much to talk about.

"She's got her ups and downs," Cal said, deciding not to share that today was definitely a down.

She winced at the news. "Well, your father will help her, don't you worry," she assured him.

"My *father?*" he asked. The certainty in her voice made him doubt anyone knew who his father truly was.

"Oh, yes," she said, with even more confidence. "She was this way before, when Vin King died. She'd refuse to leave the house for days. Got herself fired from plenty of jobs for that. If she hadn't still been living at home, she would've been forced to move back in. Your father made her right again. He was so infatuated with her. All of us who knew him from high school told him to give up, find some other girl, but he kept insisting she was the one. Your mother is lucky."

That garnered an eyeroll.

"I know I wasn't the only one who wished *my* husband was willing to devote years getting us to love ourselves again so we could love another. It was so romantic."

Another eyeroll.

"Kit," Cass's father called from downstairs.

That earned an eyeroll from Cass's mother. "He's probably going to ask where we keep the crackers," she confided to them. "You two should come down. June and her musician friend are a hoot. They seem to have endless stories to tell about Boston."

Cass and her mother argued a bit about it being crowded with the Jablonskis and Bulls showing up to see June. Cal stayed out of their squabbling, seizing the opportunity to consider this new information. Cal pondered why his mother had taken Vin's death so hard, but considering how hard she was taking Sadie's murder, concluded Ruby had done so because she'd known him, they'd still been so young, and in Vin's case, he'd had just months to go in his tour. He hadn't known his mother had been like this before, but if Milo had really snapped her out of it then, it was puzzling why he didn't return to what had worked, instead of the hapless efforts he put forth now.

"Cal?"

He turned to Cass, and saw the topic they were discussing before her mother burst in wasn't over. Cal hadn't even noticed her mother had retreated back downstairs.

"I'm not backsliding on getting out of here," she insisted. She waved at the raucousness taking place below. "I want the ability to carry a room like she does."

"How're you going to do that if you choose Dartmouth? It won't make sense to live in a dorm if you can commute from home. It'll be harder to build strong relationships when you head home every day while everyone else still has plenty of friends they can hang out with on campus."

"Look, I'm not *choosing* Dartmouth. I just . . . you saw Lance today. He was a wreck. And he was convinced all year he'd have his pick of Harvard, Yale, Princeton, you name it. I just want to keep my options open. In case we both don't get into NYU."

He shook off the idea. It was a reasonable argument, but she was talking crazy. "I'll go to Brown if that's where you get accepted," he offered as an olive branch.

She tried to flash him a reassuring smile, giving up quickly when she couldn't even convince herself. There was another burst of laughter from downstairs, and he fought down the urge to scream at them to keep it down.

The springs in her mattress shifted under her weight as she sat up. Cal closed his eyes, knowing more was coming. She only took that stance when she was preparing to deliver bad news to him, and seeing he was already upset, she must've decided she had nothing left to lose.

"What do you think about Sherman joining us for prom?"

His whole body went rigid. It was worse than he feared. "But . . . *we're* going to prom."

"I know, I know," she said, too quickly. "It's just, he asked if I had plans, and since we're going *ironically*, I figured, maybe it wouldn't be such a big deal." She looked at him, and impatient for an answer, insisted, "It's not a date!"

Cal wasn't sure if she was referring to him or Sherman. "Uh, sure. I mean, we wanted to go as a joke anyway. The more the merrier."

He didn't feel the least bit merry. They'd made the plans in the fall, both positive they wouldn't find dates that would make the experience more memorable than if they went together. At the time, it'd felt like yet another event they inevitably went to together. Only now, everything was moving so fast as they prepped themselves for the future, and seeing each other regularly looked to be in jeopardy. One of them was always working on weekends, Sherman was taking up the rest of her free time, his mother was taking up his, and Cass was growing uncertain about the colleges that might want her. Prom was fast turning into one of the few nights they had left to be together.

And now even that was being encroached upon. Everything was changing so rapidly this year, and even though he welcomed this as a necessary metamorphosis into adulthood, experiencing some of the casualties of the life he'd known was proving harder than expected.

Glancing around Cass's room, he noted how much of it had transformed over the years. The nightlight that was always plugged in when she was eight had given way to the glow in the dark constellations plastered on her ceiling. Her goldfish Cesar had been replaced by Colby. Her walls were no longer adorned with posters of teen heartthrobs she vehemently denied ever swooning over, replaced by her favorite bands and philosophers. Her bed had grown to a queen-size, her safety blanket no longer prominently displayed over sheets with the images of animated princesses. It was strange to think he'd gotten what he wanted, that they weren't kids anymore, and yet still felt a pang of remorse over it.

"Damn, you look like you fell down a well of *deep* thought."

Cal snapped back to reality to see Cass's sister June standing in the doorway. The steady stream of laughter still permeated below.

The distraction June offered was appreciated. He had no interest continuing the current conversation, and the only other topic that came to mind, bitching about Milo, was one he tried to avoid when he was alone with Cass. Cal told himself he wanted the time they were guaranteed to still have together to be joyous, but that wasn't the reason he kept his gripes to a minimum when they were alone. Cass had once asked if he was afraid of ending up like Milo. He'd said no, but even one year later, Cal believed she'd known he was lying. She'd hit the mark. He'd been afraid. And still was. Afraid that as young as he was, his whole life could spiral into Milo's if he wasn't careful. That fear was the driving force behind everything he did. Getting good grades. Expanding his horizons. Getting out of here. Being anti-Milo.

"Did Mom send you to fetch us?" Cass asked.

"God, no!" June groaned as she entered the room, shutting the door behind her.

Cal doubted their mother would mind the door being shut with both her daughters alone with him. Even he doubted he was smooth enough to woo both sisters at the same time.

"I came up here to take a break from the show Mom's making me put on."

"Aww, whatsamatter? You don't like making time for your fans, *Juniper*?" Cass teased.

She never passed up the opportunity to mock her sister's use of her full legal name for branding purposes. "Art dealers in the city don't want to buy paintings from someone who sounds like they're from bumblefuck nowhere," June had said. "But Juniper sounds exotic. International. It grabs their attention."

"I came home looking for a break from all that," June responded. "They still in the same place?" she asked, sweeping toward Cass's dresser before waiting for a nod. She dug through her sister's underwear drawer, producing a pack of cigarettes, then opened Cass's bedroom window and perched herself on the windowsill. "Mom waited until I unpacked my bags before telling me she'd invited the neighbors. She knew I would've booked a hotel if I'd known beforehand."

She savored a deep drag before blowing the smoke out the window. Her body deflated slightly as she expelled the tension outward. Sensing something in the air was amiss, June cast her discerning eyes on the two of them.

"What's going on?" she demanded. "What'd I walk into?"

"Nothing," Cal answered hurriedly, confirming her suspicions.

"We're just nervous about our consultations with Lafia," Cass lied.

June nodded as she turned to the window to exorcise another lungful of smoke. With her attention elsewhere, Cal and Cass glanced at each other before sharing a sigh of relief.

June giggled as she faced them again. "You'll have to tell me the advice he gives you, Cass, now that Sadie isn't the troubled youth this town labeled her as."

Cal was still furrowing his brow when Cass asked, "What do you mean?"

June purged another cloud of smoke out the window, halfway through the stick. "When I was your age, he gave the same spiel to all the girls. Don't end up like Sadie Grimes. He'd open our files, review them for two seconds, slam them shut, then spend the whole session barking at us about the similarities he saw between us and the troubled girl who'd gotten herself killed. Didn't matter what your school record looked like. Straight A's? Ah, but they're not A pluses. You know who else didn't have A pluses? Participating in clubs every day after school? Ah, but you've got all this free time on weekends. You know who else had endless idle time in their schedule? He even had a critique for never having detention."

"He hassled *you* over all that?" Cass asked.

"Yes, though not as bad as the other girls," June admitted. "With me, he said it was a promising start, but that I was one of the students he was most concerned about."

"Why?" Cal asked.

"Because according to him, it'd be a shame to squander that potential by showing *any* signs that I was ending up like Sadie. Like the rest of the town, he still believed she'd run away from home her senior year and gotten killed by a stranger. Mom filled me in on everything going on over the past few months. Mr. Lafia's probably fuming that he's got to find new material now."

"You think he's been using the same narrative the past decade?"

June finished off the rest of the cigarette, extinguished the end in her fingers, and let it drop to the bushes below. Her parents would continue being blissfully unaware of her habit if she retrieved the butt before they found it.

"I'd wager he's been preaching the same sermon since she first went missing, only tweaking the severity of it when her body was found." She chuckled.

"Only now that everything's come out, he can't because the whole town knows it's bullshit. She wasn't trying to escape her drunk father. There wasn't some murderous crowd she fell in with. She was just a girl who kept to herself and fell for the wrong guy."

Cass sighed, still nervous. "I doubt we'll get off as easy as you. Neither of us have a bright future preordained for us like you had. We're still hashing out all the details."

June fixed her with an odd glance. "That might be the dumbest thing I've ever heard you say, and growing up, you had some absolute gems."

"What? You were always going to become a great artist," Cass said defensively, before quickly adding, "Should your friend be left alone with Mom and Dad this long?"

"Phoenix can handle herself," June dismissed Cass's attempt to get rid of her. "What, you think my life's been a cakewalk because anyone who's ever met me has predicted what a brilliant artist I'd become? Do you have any idea how heavy it weighs on you to shoulder everyone's expectations like that?"

"June," Cal tried to cut in. "I don't think—"

"That's the problem. You don't think. Neither of you. You've both got this unshakable worldview based off zero life experiences. And the sad thing is, being so young, you don't know what you don't know. Yeah, I've got talent, more than most. But you know what? So did everyone else at Julliard. *That* was a hard fact to learn, that I didn't stand above all my peers on talent alone anymore. So, I started busting my ass to get ahead, been doing so ever since to *stay* ahead. Sure, I mix colors well, compose engaging images, but I've found myself having to do all the things I hated doing when I was your age. Getting out of my shell, standing before strangers talking about my work because as great as I believed I was, I was still a nobody in the artworld. Or negotiating prices to find that sweet spot where my stuff sold *and* I could keep the heat on in my apartment.

"You think it was easy?" she scoffed. "I don't remember it that way. I can't tell you how many times I nearly walked away from my dreams. But it was more than daily. Let me share the lesson life taught me: Your 'destiny' might be the hardest path to follow. Just ask Connor Olsen."

Two pairs of eyes stared blankly at her.

"What? You never heard of him? He was *revered* at Julliard. His surrealist paintings were better than anything I'd ever done. Probably *could* ever do. All his professors boasted about the amazing career he'd have. It got in his head. He started toking more and more to take the pressure off. He didn't have to say it. You could just tell looking at him. It wasn't fun to paint anymore. He works behind a desk now. A lot of amazing friends I made do, too. They all lost their passion.

"I kept mine, but it was a struggle. I almost dropped out my senior year." She let that hang in the air.

Neither Cal nor Cass spoke, too stunned by the admission.

"I thought maybe it'd be easier to quit, too, and settle for a quiet life like Mom and Dad. I thought *they* had to have it easier, not taking a chance on their dreams, following the simple life: get a job, marry someone, buy a house, raise some kids. I thought 'This life even comes with a blueprint.' But then Dad got laid off, and was out of work for eight months, and the two of them were scraping by on one paycheck, buried under a mortgage, taking care of a ten-year-old, I was thinking there's no way *that* was part of their plan.

"That's when it hit me. *No one's* got it *easy*. We're *all* thrown curveballs. So, I asked myself: Do I want to brave the trials life throws at me trying to be everyone else, or pursuing my dreams? It's been easier ever since I discovered my motivation. So, let my naivety be a lesson for you. It's going to be a hard path, whatever you decide to make of life. At least take the path that brings you where you want to go."

8: Late

Cal kept the car in neutral as he eased into the driveway. There were no lights on to greet him, but that didn't mean Milo wasn't waiting for him. It wasn't until he cracked the front door open and was met with warring snores coming from both ends of the house that he knew he was free of repercussions, at least for the night.

Ruby had snuck out of their bedroom after Milo had zonked out for the night. She was spooning an empty bottle of vodka on the couch. Cal hoped it was an old bottle she'd finished off tonight. He guessed her glass had rolled under the couch, making a mental note to check in the morning.

A late-night show was on now, but the local news preceded it. The drying tears on her face suggested there'd been more updates.

Cal bit back anger against himself. He should've known better than to entrust Milo with taking care of her. The coward had probably slunk to his room to focus on his work, as if another promotion with his name on it was coming along anytime soon.

"C'mon, Mom," he whispered as he gently eased her to her feet. She sank like a stone once the couch was no longer under her. "Time for bed," he said as he hoisted her into his arms, carrying her to her room.

He nearly dropped her when he stepped on something laid out on her bedroom floor. Cal's hissed curse cut through the air. Milo sawed more wood in response.

"How?" Ruby murmured as he eased her onto the bed.

"How what, Mom?" he whispered in the darkness.

Her eyes opened momentarily. She smiled drunkenly. "My prince," she said wistfully, before her eyes clamped shut with remorse. "How couldn'ah see?" she moaned. "He'did enlissst'd s'fast. Should'ahbeen obph'vious."

Cal drew the sheets over her. "Don't blame yourself, Mom." He drew a breath, convinced that would keep his voice from cracking further. "No one else saw it, either."

He turned to leave, and stepped on the same thing. Furious, he stooped down, collected the object, and stormed out of the room, chased by Milo's snores.

Cal returned to the living room and turned off the television. The vodka looked to have a few sips left. He brought it with him to the kitchen. No sense in it going to waste before throwing it out. Neither would suspect him when they found it in the trash the next morning.

As he sucked down a healthy gulp, he studied the wooden box that had threatened to break his neck twice. A small brass key hung loosely in its lock. Cal turned it, finding it stuffed to the brim with scraps of paper, most of them handwritten letters. There was no order to their arrangement, they were merely stacked haphazardly atop one another. The three on top were peppered with splotches. He frowned, recognizing they were made by his mother's tears.

"—night was amazing!" was written on the top page.

He recognized his mother's shorthand, and surmised this was an old diary entry. A splotch distorted the next few words. "—right, as usual. Date was exactly what we needed to take our minds off that poor girl's disappearance. Not a fan how got money to pay for it. Don't like the idea of stranger raising a child he'll never know. One day—"

The entry cut off as he reached the end of the page. Cal set it aside to read the next sheet.

"Ruby Baby," the next letter began, telling Cal it was a love letter. As he read the intimate letter meant only for his mother's eyes, his breath became labored.

Even marred by tears, Cal could see the note spared nothing as it vividly painted a rich tapestry in his mind of the life they'd share together.

"All the gold in the world can't compare to the Ruby I've already got." "If we have girls, they'll be the spitting image of their mother, right down to those infinitely adorable dimples." "We'll travel the world so I can showcase my queen."

It would've astonished him seeing this side of his father.

Only it wasn't Milo's handwriting.

He dropped the letter like it was cursed. With nothing else to focus on, his eyes drifted to the last paper in his hands. His blood didn't run cold, it froze completely. Although there was handwriting on it, it wasn't a note. but a medical form. From a Massachusetts fertility center. Cal recognized his mother's signature at the bottom of the page. He felt his whole body growing limp, yet his hands managed to hold the page while he kept reading. He hunted for the word DONOR on the page. He found it, only to see it was followed by NUMBER and then a string of digits that meant nothing to him.

Scouring the page, he found DONOR again, this time followed by LAST NAME. Cal threw the paper as though it were scalding. His hand brushed against the box, and something inside rattled. He gasped after his trembling hands reached inside and retrieved a half-heart locket.

Cal stared at the last name on the form.

King.

Friday

9: Morning Fog

Sleep proved elusive. Cal stared up at his ceiling, picking a higher number to count backward from, as if that was the problem. Just like the previous five attempts, before long, his mind screamed for answers. Answers he didn't have.

Were those tests real?

Cal tossed about. He felt like he was roasting, even after kicking all his sheets onto the floor. The mattress was uncomfortable no matter how many new positions he flopped into. The cool air from the window he'd opened did nothing to quell how thick and noxious it felt to breathe.

It was an out-of-state fertility center.

Did Mom tell anyone what she was doing?

He pulled his pillow over his face, convinced he'd pass out before suffocating. Neither ended up happening. He sprang to the bathroom, hunched over the toilet, only to dry heave for the third or fourth time.

Does anyone know what I am? Who I am?

Cal settled back onto his bed, assuring himself this time sleep would take him. He swore he kept his eyes shut twice, and then watched the minutes change on his digital clock seconds later. An insidious knot pulsated in the pit of his stomach, threatening to burst out of him the next time he raced to the bathroom to vomit.

Such a silly question. How can anyone know who you are? You don't even know who you are.

Slowly, he rolled onto his back, staring blankly at his ceiling, succumbing to the need to process what he'd learned about himself. His mind would not shut down with this weighing on him.

He drew up mental images of himself and Vin and compared them side by side, looking for similarities. None were obvious, but then, no one ever commented about how he looked like Milo, either. Cal analyzed the way he spoke, the way he carried himself, his social skills, academic skills, hygiene, finances, organization, religious beliefs, and cross checked everything else he could think of against the database he kept in his head on Vin King. Only a handful of attributes overlapped.

Yet he couldn't convince himself that what he read wasn't true.

His neck snapped at the blare of his alarm. He must've managed to nod off at some point during the night as his bedroom was no longer shrouded in complete darkness, and he couldn't recall the early rays of dawn gradually sleeping in.

He climbed out of bed, the knot in his gut continuing to bubble, threatening an eruption at any moment. Every step felt weighted as he struggled with his morning routine. Whereas most days he could run on autopilot, this morning proved a challenge. Twice, he caught himself standing outside of the shower watching the room fill with steam. What to do with the shampoo bottle in his hand was a conundrum. And when dressing, he had to take off his shoes after realizing he was only wearing one sock.

The long shower did nothing to ease his pounding head. The world looked like it'd been run through a sepia filter. Everything looked familiar, yet foreign to him, like he was moving through an interactive replica of his entire life.

Cal had no idea how long he'd been staring at the television before he realized he'd turned it on. The sound was muted as the screen cut from news anchors to an image of the field Sadie had been buried in. Faded Rogan Construction signs still hadn't been taken down.

The updates he craved every morning now sickened him. He found the coverage of the murder extremely biased. The cause of death had been determined as blunt force trauma to the base of her skull. On its face, it looked horrible, but maybe the deed wasn't as malicious as it appeared. The field had its share of boulders jutting from the ground. Perhaps he'd only meant to shove her away, and she'd lost her balance. It was unfortunate, but not premeditated. Maybe he had nothing to do with her death. Maybe she just tripped.

"Some milk would go good with that," a voice said, interrupting his tangle of thought.

He twisted to see Milo had entered the kitchen from the hallway. Cal glanced down at a bowl of cereal he couldn't remember pouring. From a great distance, Milo tssked his disapproval over what Cal was watching. Cal switched the television off without protest.

Milo breezed through his morning routine with his left hand while he studied a stack of forms in his right.

He gave no indication he'd noticed Cal watching his every move until he'd taken his first sip of coffee.

"Son?"

Cal flinched at the title.

Milo stiffened his lip at Cal's reaction, but continued as though it didn't bother him. "Something on your mind?"

For once, Cal didn't roll his eyes at one of Milo's understated questions. All he wanted to do was scream *Yes*, that he had hundreds of questions, possibly millions, and was poised to rain them down on Milo. Cal wished he hadn't returned Ruby's wooden box of keepsakes to their bedroom. He'd done so because he didn't want to look at it, but now he longed to show it to them to get an explanation. About everything. One question haunted him above all others. Did Milo know? If Milo was as in the dark as Cal was yesterday, he'd be no closer to getting answers. The uncertainty stayed his tongue, even with Milo staring at him, awaiting a reply.

"I've got to go," Cal said and left without another word.

He thought it nothing short of a miracle that he ended up at school. He wandered through the crowded halls aimlessly, getting lost twice before he found his locker and was able to orient himself, but blanked on his locker combination. He gave up on it, and meandered in the direction he guessed his homeroom was in. It wasn't until he noticed Jamie opening his own locker that he realized he'd staggered in the wrong direction.

The sight of the sophomore's bare locker caught his attention. The kid *had* emptied it out yesterday. The only thing left was a family picture taped to the inside of the door. After looking up and down the hall, Jamie peeled it off delicately, taking care to preserve it in his hollow book bag, gave one last resigned look at the barren compartment, and closed it. He didn't even put the lock back on.

Cal was about to ask if Jamie was moving out of town when Jamie's head jerked toward some joyous hooting. Cal turned to see classmates parting in the hallway to avoid being trampled by Milton and his cronies. When Cal turned back, Jamie was bolting the other way, weaving through the crowd before he was spotted.

Cal squirmed in his seat throughout homeroom, scratching nervously up and down his arms and legs. He was confused why no one else was affected by the dense air. The whole room carried on like any other Friday, but now he felt trapped listening to kids ramble about the latest news coverage of Sadie's murder.

He did his best to ignore the juicy gossip that an anonymous fertility clinic employee had leaked the news that Vin had made a donation for cash twenty-five years ago, instead focusing his attention intently on two jocks hoping the Sox could salvage the rough start to the season against their rivals this weekend.

The urge to leave was palpable by first period. The thick air had become suffocating, and his mind was hammering against his skull. His short, heavy breaths drew constant, irritated stares. Cal was oblivious, his comatose stare fixed on no particular spot of the dry erase board.

After contemplating all morning, Cal concluded the manner of Sadie's death didn't change things. Even if her demise had been nothing more than misfortune, Vin had hidden her body. Being a scared teenager who feared guilt would be assigned to him didn't excuse his actions. He'd denied her father closure. He fled from town as soon as he could. He never once came forward and explained what happened.

No matter the circumstances, Vin King was evil.

It took Mr. Pendergrass shouting his name to snap Cal out of his thoughts. Cal replied to all his questions with the same shrug, then receded back within himself, leaving Mr. Pendergrass to fix him with a disappointed shake of the head before moving on.

Cal followed suit when everyone got up from their seats. He hadn't heard the bell going off. It was only when he packed up that he noticed the swelling claw marks up and down his forearms. As hard as he'd dug into his skin, he was no closer to uncovering what was crawling all over him.

It was the same routine for his next two classes, sitting silently, lost in his own thoughts, only moving when everyone else got up. Cal only snapped out of it when gentle yet firm hands gripped his shoulders. He turned to see Zell regarding him with a quizzical look.

"Hey, man. Did you forget your appointment with Lafia?"

10: Escape

Cal couldn't place the name of the junior fidgeting nervously in the waiting area. Her eyes leaped to Cal as he ripped the office door open, pleading with him that everything she'd heard about Mr. Lafia was blown out of proportion as a way to scare juniors. Whatever she saw in Cal wasn't reassuring. Her face could've sunk into the basement.

He disregarded her the same way he did the voice demanding he come back. Cal stormed out of the guidance counselor's office, slamming the door behind him. He thought he heard stacks of papers being blown from the desks by the gale force wind he'd created.

A wall clock told him there was still ten minutes left of the period. He had no intention of making that class, or any desire to attend the rest. Cal fell in line behind a group of students coming in from outside. If the hall monitor paid attention, she would've noticed Cal was the only one not in gym shorts and demanded to see his hall pass. She only spared them a glance, and once they rounded the corner, Cal split off.

He still wasn't sure where he was going when he spotted Jamie coming out of the bathroom.

Jamie halted, confused as to why Cal was scrutinizing him.

Movement in Cal's peripherals caught his attention. When Jamie didn't budge, Cal realized the sophomore hadn't spotted them yet. He opened his mouth to scream a warning, but before he could—

"Look who it is," Milton hollered.

Jamie's eyes froze in terror. He glanced over his shoulder, back into the bathroom. Cal's eyes begged him not to retreat into the restroom. He'd be trapping himself. When Jamie turned back around, Cal could see he'd drawn the same conclusion.

The decision cost him, all the same. By the time he took flight down the hallway, Milton had grabbed his shoulder, yanking him off his feet.

"What're ya doin' in the *boy's* room?" Milton demanded, planting a kick in his ribs. "Didja wanna see what a *real* pecker looked like? Or were ya just hopin' to suck one?"

Balled up in a sitting fetal position, Jamie's terrified eyes turned to Cal for help before Milton's cronies advanced on him, swallowing him up from Cal's view.

Cal watched blankly, unsure of what to do as they started landing their kicks.

The goons stopped when they heard buzzing. Cal's vibrating phone broke the spell he was under. Milton was the first to turn around and acknowledge he was still there.

"Keep walking," Milton barked.

Jamie was visible again. Tears poured down his face, but there was no signs of bruises or blood. The thugs were wise enough to beat him without leaving any marks.

"*Hey!*" Milton shouted, now taking a step toward Cal. "I told ya to scram."

The tone didn't sit well with Cal. Piled atop the relentless hammering in his skull, the nauseous bile percolating in his stomach, and the way something was still scampering across and under his skin, he'd reached his breaking point. He'd still been wrapping his head around who his father was, and his meeting with Lafia had only exacerbated everything. He was furious, and Milton was looking for a fight, too.

"Leave him alone." He didn't recognize his voice.

"What'd you say?" Milton hissed.

He fixed Cal with a vicious scowl, but it was too late. There'd been a moment's hesitation before he'd responded, and they both knew the others had noticed.

There was a pause before Cal replied. But this was deliberate. "Leave. Him. Alone."

The harder Milton tried to hide it, the more Cal could see the uncertainty in his eyes, even as he closed the gap on Cal. His cronies were watching behind him. He couldn't afford to back down.

"What, is he yer *boyfriend*?" Milton snarled.

He shoved Cal hard into the wall of lockers. The thug's eyes widened when Cal's fist connected squarely with his jaw. The brute's head rocked back, his legs tripped over themselves, sending him sailing backward. Milton moaned from the floor. Even though they were shielded behind a wall of tears, Cal could still make out the horrific shock in Milton's eyes, giving the impression no one have ever fought back before. Cal was equally astounded. He'd never thrown a punch before.

Milton cradled his jaw like his hand was the only thing keeping it in place. A purple knot was already bulging along his cheek, and his fingertips had reddened. Cal had busted his lip open.

Jamie scuttled across the floor as Milton's cronies turned their attention from him. The rest of the gang closed in on Cal, ready to avenge their leader, freezing when their target turned his sights on them. Cal had no idea what they saw in his eyes, but whatever it was, it did the trick. Any thoughts of vengeance drained from their faces. Cal could feel their strength sapping. They stooped down to check on Milton, trying to play it off that they weren't terrified, merely concerned for their leader.

Cal decided not to press his luck. He charged through the closest door that took him outside and just kept walking. It felt satisfying standing up to a menace like Milton.

His smile wilted when he thought of how many times Vin might have raised his fists to solve his problems.

His vibrating phone made him aware Cass had messaged him a few times, wanting to know if he'd seen Lance this morning because he wasn't in Chemistry. Cal had no idea if he'd seen him this morning. Everything today had melted into a blur. Slugging Milton felt a surreal daydream.

A sharp gust of wind picked up, biting his exposed skin. His arms stung the worst, and when he examined them, he saw the meeting with Lafia had pushed his clawing to the point where he'd drawn blood.

Cass kept texting, wanting to know where he was. Cal had no idea himself. He'd wandered around aimlessly for hours, chased by questions he was afraid to answer. He scanned his surroundings for a clue, then typed his location.

"Ur downtown?!" was the immediate reply. The font would've been italicized if his phone allowed it.

Cal ignored the question, as well as the litany of texts that followed. He collapsed onto a nearby bench on Main Street, giving his exhausted feet a break. He tried to take his mind off Lafia by people-watching, focusing on a derelict stationed between the bank and neighboring grocery store, holding a cardboard sign. She eventually earned enough to enter the grocer's, but once she emerged with a cheap bottle of rum, she looked content, sitting against the wall of the grocer, only taking a break from sucking down the rum to caw at passersby to spare some change.

Boredom started to set in, even when another derelict, a man in similar ratty, baggy, holey rags, caked in filth like she was, materialized next to her and immediately admonished her. Meandering about hadn't cleansed his mind of what Lafia said. He desperately needed another distraction, and after staring at the bank for so long, Cal was convinced with enough cash in hand, he'd find one.

"Gabs, things don't pick up because you don't want them to," the irate derelict explained as Cal drew near.

"Pah!" Gabs spat at his feet. "You think I'm here cuz I *want* to be, Randy? That I'm choosin' the fine cuisine of the soup kitchens over restaurants? That I prefer spendin' my days holdin' this sign, wonderin' which'd be worse, that my old friends recognized me, or didn't?"

While they were preoccupied with one another, Cal lowered his head and charged for the bank's entrance. He fumbled for the front door, worried that if he looked up, Gabs would caw at him.

"Gabs, I know things're takin' awhile to develop," Randy stated calmly, "but once they get going, everything'll takeoff at once. I told ya, baby, I'm making moves. George'll have some construction work for me now that it's warming up again. We just gotta keep working the plan, work harder than the rest of the dullards in this town who frit away their lives. In no time, it'll be *you* looking down on your old friends when you see them."

"Grand plans," Gabs muttered. "Always grand plans."

Cal breathed a sigh of relief once he was safely inside, then got irritated when the teller's suspicious eyes gave him the once-over, accusing him of skipping school.

He rashly drained his account and closed it.

It should have terrified him watching his entire savings placed before him. That was money for his first car, his ticket to freedom after graduation. Instead, he smirked. Vin had never had half as much to his name at any one time. The euphoria didn't last. Wealth, like poverty, wasn't a characteristic, only a circumstance. That sentiment was chased by the thought that Cal wasn't the only one who'd had plans to flee this town and never look back.

The texts escalated to calls as he pocketed the fresh bills. He skimmed through her disregarded texts, picking up on the increasing anguish in her messages. I'm OK, he typed back simply, then continued on his pilgrimage to nowhere in particular.

The derelicts were still preoccupied with one another when he emerged from the bank. He grinned, thinking they had no idea how much money they'd never get by allowing him to slip away.

"If you'd just stop blowing your half of our earnings," Randy said in a huff.

"Pah! You got a *better* way of escapin' this nightmare?" Gabs challenged.

"How many times do I keep telling you, we need all the money we can get by Monday."

By her fifth missed call, Cal realized Cass had also abandoned her regular school schedule. He contemplated turning his phone off, but knew that would send her into hysterics. Reluctantly, he answered.

"*Oh, thank God,*" she cried, exasperated. Her voice sounded like she'd been struggling to hold back tears. "*Talk to me.*" In the background, Cal heard Zell asking if he was with Lance.

"I'm fine," Cal said flatly.

"*Why'd you leave?*"

"I just . . . you know. I couldn't stand to be there another minute. You know?"

"*No! I don't know!*"

Cal couldn't blame her for yelling. He wasn't making any sense to himself, either. "I just . . . I can't explain. Not over the phone." He trusted she'd known him long enough to pick up his hint. He started surveying the area.

"*So, come back, and let's talk.*"

In the background, Zell was asking what they were talking about.

The school day would almost be over by the time he returned. Regardless, he didn't want to risk the slightest chance of hearing the latest about Vin King. His eyes settled on an ideal location.

"No. Meet me at Down the Hatch."

"*You're at a—*"

Her voice cut off when he hung up.

11: Down the Hatch

Even though he'd been a patron numerous times, his whole body tensed up at the thought of entering the bar. Every time he'd been here, it'd been a Saturday night, well past the dark of midnight, when the place was slammed, the bartender and bouncer both weary from long shifts they were counting down. Cal wasn't confident his fake ID would pass inspection under the light of day. He sidled up alongside two passersby talking baseball when entering the tavern as though they were all together.

"Hey!" the bartender yelled as soon as he crossed the threshold of the bar.

Cal froze in terror.

"Paul. *Paul!* Change the channel!" a barfly squealed at the bartender, hopping in his seat.

The two baseball fans he'd entered with, seeing the drunk making a scene, diverted their trajectory to the other side of the bar's counter. After a moment, Cal followed suit, fearing he'd attract attention if he stood there dumbfounded. He spared the bartender a glance, relieved that he was preoccupied with the hopping wino.

"In a *minute*, Chester," Paul said gruffly as he sauntered to the barfly, his back turned to Cal.

"He's on the screen!" Chester went manic when Paul didn't hustle to his liking. Cal glanced at the small screen mounted in the corner of the bar to see what was agitating Chester so severely.

"*It's important we don't turn our backs on those who need us most.*" Morris was speaking before a pack of reporters. He and one reporter were engaged in a tug o' war over possession of the microphone held closest to him.

Apprehension gripped Cal's throat and heart simultaneously. The constant stream of updates about the murder was inescapable.

"Oh, shut it!" Chester screamed at the screen, before spitting at the image.

The reporter was slowly pulling the mic away from Morris, who in turn, continued leaning in as he spoke. "*Anyone can judge a person at their lowest. But few take the time putting themselves in another's shoes, to understand why they've fallen through bottomless pits.*"

"*Chester!*" Paul roared. "What'd I tell you about spittin' in my bar!"

"*I know what it's like,*" Morris stated, as though he was the only one who *could* understand what "they" were going through. "*I used to be them.*" On screen, Morris gave the mic a jerk, failing to wrench it from the reporter's grasp.

"We all preferred you that way!" Chester screamed at the television. He picked up his half-drunk pint, ready to fling it at the screen. Most of it spilled down his arm, prompting him to salvage what was left and drain it in one pull. "Wouldja change the channel already?" He was vibrating at an intense frequency, looking poised to tear the bar down with his bare hands if he had to listen to Morris much longer.

Cal felt his cell vibrating. When he saw it wasn't Cass, he ignored it.

Paul emphatically pressed buttons on the remote. Morris' image remained on screen.

"*That's why I trek around the northeast, sharing my story,*" Morris continued, as the mic slowly pulled away again. "*You all* do *have my schedule?*" he turned to the reporters to ask.

There was a chorus of murmured yeses.

"*And you'll all be posting my tour dates?*"

Another refrain of weary affirmatives.

"Hurry!" Chester bellowed to Paul.

"Damn batteries must've died. Sit tight," he instructed as he stepped out from behind the bar, and disappeared into an office.

Chester stewed on his stool, struggling with an advanced case of the shakes.

"*Just wanted to make sure,*" Morris said, his words soaked with self-importance. "*Plenty of fine organizations are paying me well to speak. I want to make sure I'm doing my part, ensuring I'm speaking to full houses so they're getting their money's worth.*"

That sent Chester over the edge. "You'd make an even greater fortune collectin' money from people wantin' you to *shut up!*"

"Chester! Heel!" Paul commanded as he breezed back behind the bar, batteries in hand.

"*It's important to hear experiences from someone who used to be one of them,*" Morris prattled on. "*Sulking over endless pints about the state of my life. Never taking action to change. My Sadie going missing should've pushed me over the edge. Hearing how the town viewed her, and* me, *should've broken me. Yet, here I stand. God may not've held up* His *end of the bargain to return my Sadie safe and sound, but I've been true to my vows of never touching another drink.*"

"'Stead of sobriety, you should've offered God a vow of silence!" Chester howled.

"*Heel*, Chester," Paul snapped. "The batteries're in."

"*Miss,*" Morris fixed one of the reporters offscreen with a tone. "*If you'll please stop pulling the mic away from me. I don't wish for your viewers to suffer with any sound issues because they can't hear my—*"

Chester slumped on his stool with a relieved grunt as the image changed to some rerun. The TV remained on the channel for only a moment before the baseball fan closest to Cal requested it be changed to the game. Hearing the interest in the night's game, Chester perked up and drew a deep breath, about to spew longwinded unsolicited opinions.

Paul, for his part, spared his potential well-paying customers from suffering Chester's soliloquy. "You and Morris aren't mending fences anytime soon?" Paul chided gently.

"I don't even know him anymore!" Chester grumbled, mercifully distracted. "He acts like gettin' piss drunk with me was the worst times of his life. The way he talks, it's like he looks down on the likes of me."

Paul nodded as he meandered over to the two baseball fans and Cal, shifting his attention to them while Chester rambled on. Cal tensed up now that the bartender was looking at him. Cal had strategically positioned himself within arm's length of the other two. At a glance he'd still look to be a member of their party, but to them, he'd just be someone who took the empty seat closest to them. Now, under the scrutiny of Paul's gaze, Cal wished he'd tried to join the conversations of any of the other patrons who hadn't come directly to the counter.

"It's Charles, right?" Paul finally broke the silence.

Cal did his best to exhale evenly so his relief wasn't obvious. The bartender had not only remembered him, but the name on the driver's license he'd used to order drinks. "My friends call me Chuck," he corrected.

"Right," the bartender said with a nod. "Where's that girl of yours?"

"Oh, Zelda should be coming when she gets off work," Cal said, completely at ease now.

He ordered "the usual" without even attempting to produce the bogus license. Cal knew the odd coupling of names was the reason the bartender remembered him and Cass. The whole tavern had teased them about it the first time they'd tested their fake IDs. They took it good-naturedly. There was no sense making a fuss over the ribbing if it meant they could keep drinking all night.

"You're a lager man, right?"

Despite how smoothly things were going, Cal couldn't shake the feeling the bartender still suspected he was underage, and that the question was a trap. "Stouts," he rectified, even though he wasn't sure what they tasted like.

"What'd I ever do, 'cept prop him up the whole walk home, made sure he got through his front door so's he didn't freeze to death?" Chester jabbered incessantly while Paul poured. "And I ain't never been nothin' but supportive. Bringing food t'make sure he was eatin' when Sadie first went missin' 'cause he was an absolute wreck. Hell, I even steered him toward the diner one time when I saw him heading this way after Sadie'd been found."

Cal gave Paul a knowing eyeroll, drawing a smirk. Cal felt it best to further win Paul's confidences by presenting himself as someone who'd dealt with the likes of Chester as well.

Chester started repeating himself. "I did nothin' but support him. Anytime he lost his job for comin' in shitfaced too many days, I was there to console him. Anytime he got a new job, I bought the first round. And when he vowed he'd never drink again if his Sadie returned safe and sound, well, I was blue over potentially losin' my best drinkin' buddy, but if it meant his girl would turn up okay, I'd make that trade. Now he goes around, pretendin' he's givin' speeches to help drunks like he used to be. But that ain't it. I can see it in his eyes every time he's on TV. He looks down on us, people like me. Only when we've sworn off booze does he stop regardin' us as vermin."

Déjà vu struck Cal's taste buds hard, reminding him of the first beer he, Zell, Lance, and Cass had shared. He fought back the urge to spit it out this time. His façade as a seasoned drinker who knew what he wanted would crumble immediately if he showed distaste in a drink he claimed to love.

The door began openly more frequently as people were making the bar their first stop of the weekend. Many wore something with the Sox logo on it. Cal's frown deepened each time a group of strangers entered. Chester continued to babble, even after Cal had finished his second beer. Cal wasn't sure when it had happened, but the drunk was now fondly reminiscing about the good times he and Morris had had getting piss drunk. Forgetting points they were making while in the middle of drunken philosophizing. Treating the jukebox like a karaoke machine.

Throwing peanuts in each other's gaping mouths when they passed out at the bar.

Cal was grateful that he had a tendency to go deaf as he drank.

As Chester's voice joined the muffled haze of the crowded chatter around him, Cal experienced a sense of euphoria that had nothing to do with the third stout he was working on. With his hearing muted, he realized he couldn't listen to any discussion of Vin King's crime. He'd found his distraction. A grin split his face, the first he'd managed since late last night, but it wasn't meant to last. Left to his inner voice, all he could focus on was the first thought he'd had when he and Cass had successfully ordered their first drinks here.

"I'll bet Milo would never do this," he muttered aloud.

The habit of obsessing over Milo's every action and mannerism was exposed as the waste it'd always been. It made no difference if he found similarities between himself and his fa—himself and Milo. Any resemblance had been pure coincidence. And recalling his comparisons to Milo led to dwelling on what Lafia had said.

Cal didn't want to think about it. Not ever, but he would settle for not now, and he knew the only way to avoid doing so was to get out of his own head. He swiveled his neck to the two baseball fans, engrossed in a passionate discussion, eyes glued to the TV.

"Who's playing?"

Both of them jumped. Cal paled, aware he'd spoken louder than he'd intended. His face drained further when they inspected him, fearing they recognized him for a minor and would tattle to Paul.

"The Sox, kid," one of them answered.

Cal's face blanched further, convinced he'd been found out.

"Who're gonna get their rears kicked by New York," the other added. Some nearby Sox fans booed him, which drew an impish smile. "And their victory will be all the sweeter once Tommy here loses another bet to me."

"Logan, you're not—"

"That Clark kid is gonna get this new manager fired as well," Chester blared from the other end of the counter, having heard the topic of baseball spring up again and wanting to join in. "Not that *he's* any better than the guy the organization paraded in last year, don't go believing that's what *I* believe."

While the two fans reacted to the interruption, Logan smirking into his mug while Tommy glared at Chester for cutting him off, they continued the conversation as though the drunk wasn't still prattling. Which he was, even with no one listening.

"Even a drunk like Chester can see that bum is dragging the team down," Logan observed wryly. He saw that earned chuckles from the nearby Sox fans who'd booed him, and turned to address them. "It's shocking to think Tommy might have less sense than our loud friend over there."

"Oh, Log." Tommy sighed good-naturedly. "You never let up, do you? Why do you keep insisting he's the root cause of the Sox's woes? He's been in the top three of every offensive category the last two years."

"What'd I tell you?" Logan worked the crowd. "*This* fool here keeps thinking that bum Clark will actually deliver a big hit for them late, to win a game."

Their response signaled to Cal that Tommy's faith in Clark was misplaced.

"Why do you believe in—hiccup—him, if he's not that good?" Cal asked Tommy, trying to control his voice so that he didn't shout, abandoning his efforts when he heard himself hiccup. From his limited experience, Cal knew this was stage two on his way to becoming drunk.

"He's got great numbers," Tommy said, grimacing in the face of Cal's shouting.

"Numbers don't tell the whole story," Logan replied.

"It's baseball. The whole game is numbers," Tommy insisted.

"To the untrained eye, Rob Clark looks like an amazing player. And for the first six innings, he truly is, putting up gaudy figures," Logan conceded. "But the statistics don't show how he performs in the later innings of close games. Who here hasn't at some point believed Clark was going to come through in the clutch, only to watch in dismay as he made an out again and again?"

Logan's question earned nods from the rest of the Sox fans.

"He's belted some homers late in games," Tommy said.

"Those hits always came in games that were already decided," Logan replied. "Go back and watch any game where his hit could've tied the score or put them ahead after the sixth. You'll find your golden boy doesn't have a single homer in those pressure situations."

"That's because other teams keep running their best relievers out to face him in close games," Tommy responded, completely exasperated that a bar full of fellow fans were siding with Logan. "If other managers are countering his at bats with their finest pitchers, shouldn't that tell you something about Rob Clark's greatness?"

"When he's always been bested in those spots, shouldn't it tell *you* something?" Logan countered.

"Al—hic—ways?" Cal asked, attempting to mumble to control his volume.

"Always," Logan said, failing to hide his displeasure at Cal's failure. "There are four inevitabilities in life. Death. Taxes. Rob Clark choking in a big spot. And Tommy losing when he gambles."

"He's never won a bet before?" Cal asked, this time completely forgetting to lower his voice until they'd recoiled.

"*C'mon*," Tommy whined, wilting slightly now that people were watching them. "You're bound to lose *one* of these times. I've been salivating for this game all week."

Cal retreated from the conversation, turning back to stare into his pint glass. He'd been too preoccupied beefing up his college transcript over the past two years to follow the sport, and even before that he'd never shown much of an interest, yet he'd enjoyed the discussion because the topic had been anything other than the murder of Sadie Grimes. Or fathers. But as with everything in his life, even this conversation became tainted when Logan had brought up certainties, once again causing his thoughts to circle back to everything he'd done to not end up like his father, and that it had all been for naught.

In search of another distraction, Cal inspected his phone, scrolling through a plethora of missed calls. None had been from Cass. He was about to call when a looming shadow swallowed him. He crooked his neck toward its source.

"You missed a lot at school today," Cass said in a controlled seethe. "Zell told me one of Milton's cronies pulled off a coup: His gang gave him a wedgie in the locker room. Zell also said Milton already had the fat lip, and that the rumor going around was you gave it to him."

Cal could tell by her fury that she wanted him to deny it. He caved under the ferocity of her glare. "That was me," Cal confessed softly.

She let him suffer under her biting gaze a while longer before breaking the silence. "What's gotten into you?"

12: Lafia

There had been nothing to look at while waiting outside for his session to begin except the exterior of Mr. Lafia's office walls. At one point, Lafia had been able to peer out the windows into the lobby where Cal was waiting, and vice versa, but now the Plexiglas was completely covered, adorned with four decades worth of news articles commending him throughout his career.

There was no apparent order to the way they'd been displayed. Articles and photographs were just plastered over what was already exhibited, giving the wall of recognition a cramped vibe. To Cal, the office wall was nothing more than a refrigerator belonging to proud hoarder parents.

(hiccup)

Although he'd clearly aged, all the photographs of him accepting awards looked the same. He adopted the same pose, arms crossed (even when he was holding a plaque), head crooked slightly down so his beak of a nose pointed toward the floor, his vulture eyes fixed directly at the camera. And that scowl. There wasn't a trace of a smile in any of the pictures.

Forty years of images glaring at Cal had only amplified the jackhammering inside his skull. Closing his eyes failed to alleviate the pounding. With no other option, he passed the time reading some of the articles. Most of them harped on how long he'd been counseling students. Plenty offered in-depth analyses of his career, charts, and graphs accompanying the articles showing the school's excellent graduation rate under his stewardship, as well as the average GPA of graduates being the highest in the state.

He was in the middle of studying a bar graph analyzing the percentage of Mr. Lafia's students who attended college after graduating compared to other schools when Lafia's door opened. The student's eyes were glazed over as she lurched out the office like a zombie. Cal assured himself her streaks of gray hair were merely a trick of the light.

(hiccup hiccup hiccup)

(Drink some water, Cal)

"Fischer," a voice called from the office. Light seemed unable to penetrate the entrance of Lafia's office, creating a shuddering sensation that the grave voice within was beckoning him into a cave, one that if he entered, he would not be the same once he emerged. If he emerged at all.

"Fischer," the voice repeated, a tinge of irritation. Cal scurried inside. He didn't dare aggravate the voice further.

Cal froze when he saw him. Though he'd been perusing photographs of the man aging over the past forty decades, seeing the man in the flesh spooked him. Witnessing him actually moving made the pictures he'd been studying more terrifying than illustrations he'd seen of horrific beasts from various mythologies. Those monsters had merely been legends. The one before him was real.

He barely had time to observe that Lafia's scalp had finally shed the last remaining traces of hair, and that his pallid skin was sagging everywhere, signs that, although the monster was frightening, it was also dying, when Lafia ensnared him in his vulture eyes. The nausea stewing in the pit of Cal's stomach intensified from a simmer to boiling over.

"Sit down, Fischer," Lafia commanded, then pointed to a nearby trashcan. "You won't be the first student to vomit in front of me. Or the last."

Cal's trembling legs gave out on him, and he crashed into the seat more than sat. His body chilled at the idea Mr. Lafia could read his thoughts.

"I've reviewed your file," Lafia began, taking it from the top of a stack of manila folders on his desk. He opened it briefly, then snapped it shut. "On the surface, it looks like you've really been applying yourself. Particularly this year."

"Thank you," Cal mumbled.

"Don't mumble. And don't thank me, either. I had nothing to do with it."

Cal disagreed. The trepidation Lafia inspired in the student body provided plenty of motivation to excel at school. Plenty of kids grew up being told by their older siblings, sometimes parents, that Mr. Lafia was the boogeyman, that he would get them if they didn't get their grades up. He didn't dare correct the man.

(I need a drink)

(Cal)

(I need a drink to get through this)

"Only three clubs."

Cal couldn't tell if it was an observation or a question. When Mr. Lafia merely sat there silently, regarding him with those vulture eyes, Cal responded, "Yes, sir. Three."

"I know it's three," Lafia snapped. "I just read it."

Cal stiffened under Lafia's critical gaze. His scrutiny had a way of making Cal's bones squirm.

"I'm concerned about your future, Fischer," Mr. Lafia eventually broke the silence.

Cal didn't know whether to be relieved or fearful that Lafia had begun talking again. This time he remained mute, believing this was the way to avoid Mr. Lafia's wrath.

"Well? Say something!" Lafia demanded.

"What concerns you?" Cal asked, his heart pounding as fast as his head. It would be a photo finish to see which exploded first.

"I'm getting strong indications you're peaking too early," Mr. Lafia pontificated. "You challenged yourself with an aggressive course load for a junior. However, you've only opted for two courses with college credits next year and three advanced placement classes."

Cal couldn't tell if this was another question he was expected to answer. He opted to nod, thinking it could be interpreted as either agreement or an indication to continue.

"Some of your classmates who've had similar classes to yours are taking double the classes that earn college credits next year. *And* they participate in more extracurriculars, too."

"Not all of them have part-time jobs like me, though," Cal defended himself.

Cal expected Lafia's flared nostrils would shoot flames. He bowed his head in apologetic subservience for the interruption. A drop of water landed on his jeans. He hadn't realized how profusely he'd been sweating.

"Your complacency is what's most alarming. You've certainly made a habit of retreating into the path of least resistance. Always doing the bare minimum to get decent grades."

Cal kept waiting for Lafia to unhinge his jaw and finish him off. He forced himself to look the counselor in his predatory eyes for an explanation of how he'd known.

"Unlike you, I go above and beyond in my duties. I confer with the teachers of the students I provide guidance to. Some of the descriptions of your behavior are downright shameful. Mrs. McCauley could only tell me you don't make any trouble for her. Mr. Pendergrass made a point to tell me you're too busy working on other assignments to participate in classroom discussions. And that you gave him an attitude when he confronted you about it."

(hic)

(Finish the story)

"You're on the outskirts of very dangerous territory," Lafia warned. "You remind me of a student who used to walk these halls. He *also* stopped applying himself, like *you're* doing," the counselor crooked an accusatory finger at Cal. "Left himself with few options after graduating by the skin of his teeth. Didn't heed my advice when I cautioned him he was squandering his potential. He was a bitter young man, I remember that. He wasn't dealt the best hand, born into a life of scarcity, one of several mouths that needed feeding. Perhaps he felt the world had treated him unkindly. I always believed that was why he enlisted, as a way to unleash his pent-up aggression. I had no idea he'd already succumbed to his own depraved inclinations before he graduated."

Mr. Lafia looked away as though he accepted personal responsibility for that student's fate. The vulture eyes were back on Cal soon enough.

"I always wonder if he could've made something of himself if he'd just tried." Lafia framed it like he was confiding in Cal, like he was the only one who could be trusted. "It's imperative that you don't repeat his mistakes. You have so much more than he ever could've dreamed for himself. You're above the poverty line. You've created opportunities for yourself with your grades. You'd be even more tragic than he was if you throw your life away by continuing down the path you're on."

(Cal)

(Hmm?)

(You stopped talking. Was that it?)

(. . . no)

(What else)

(hiccup)

(What did Mr. Lafia say?)

"But if you keep this up, you'll be following in his footsteps," Lafia cautioned. His sigh sounded sympathetic, but his malicious eyes looked as spiteful as ever.

Cal sat speechless as the counselor leaned in.

"You must stop allowing yourself to become Vin King."

13: Guts

"*That's* why you gave your brain the day off today?" Cass asked.

Cal buried his eyes in his palms. He knew his face was crumpling, but didn't want her to see him crying. He doubted she'd ever seen Sherman cry.

Her hand felt soft as she gently patted his back. "Cal, Mr. Lafia just has a way of getting inside our heads. You can't take it to heart. June didn't, and look—Cal, don't order another. You've had enough."

Cal kept his hand up until Paul came for his order. "You okay, Chuck?"

"Just allergies," Cal lied. "A round for the two of us."

"No, thanks," Cass said, firmly.

Cal rolled his watery eyes. "I'll have both, then."

Cass gasped when Cal pulled out his wallet. "How long've you been walking around with all that cash?"

"Not sure anymore," he said with a shrug, and plunked down enough to cover the drink. "Keep the change," he said to Paul.

Paul's enthusiasm informed him he'd just tipped very generously. Cass fumed while she waited for Paul to pour the drink and leave. Cal snapped his attention back to Cass when she slapped his arm. Her icy glared burned into his eyes.

"I don't understand why you're doing this. So what that Lafia equated you to Vin King?"

"Vin King is my dad," he blurted out. He froze, hearing his confession uttered aloud. The only thing he dared to move was his eyes, which darted around the bar conspiratorially to see if anyone else had heard. They all went about their conversations.

"What?" Cass asked, with a nervous chuckle. She thought it was a joke, until he met her eyes. "But . . . but how could that—"

"Found the records when I got home from your place."

The two of them sat silently, neither knowing what to say.

The surrounding babble caught Cal's attention, and glancing around, he wished he could partake in the good times everyone else seemed to be enjoying. His mind was foggy from the beers, but he surmised most of the patrons were discussing the baseball game they couldn't pull their eyes from. Only Chester's bleating penetrated the muteness his ears had transformed the bar's white noise into. Cal was growing increasingly certain that if he wasn't in his usual state of drunk deaf, Chester's voice would be audible even when he was in the bathroom taking a leak.

"It doesn't matter," Cass finally spoke. "Have you forgotten the lengths you've gone through not to turn into Milo? You succeeded when you made it your mission not to become your father once. You can do it again."

"I didn't accomplish anything," Cal remarked glumly. "It's been easy being nothing like Milo because he was never my father. The whole time I thought I was choosing not to be Milo . . . . How do I know every action didn't come naturally because I was always acting like my *real* dad?" His pint was on the verge of shattering under his tight grip. "It's like some cruel joke life is torturing me with, giving me what I wanted in the worst way."

He had enough presence of mind to sense the whole tavern deflate to something happening on television. Only Logan was hooting with delight, reveling in the hisses from the rest of the crowd. For a moment, Cal found it comforting that so many others would be miserable alongside him, but noted how quickly they reacclimated to their previous state of pleasure. Cal longed to join them there, and copied them in taking large gulps from his pint. He frowned (or tried to, he could feel the inebriated grin he always made when he'd passed his limit) when he felt no different, and waved for Paul.

"You sure that's a good idea?" Cass didn't pose it as a question. Or a suggestion. It was a dare.

Cal was up for the challenge. "My best one today."

"Probably is. The bar's not that high," she snarled. "You can't drown your problems in a bottle. They always resurface."

Cal saw the scorn that had been in her eyes when she'd first come in was nothing compared to the melting rage that was present now. "You're making a scene," she said through bared teeth.

The sensation of eyes on him got him to bolt upright on his stool. He glanced around nervously, exerting himself to look sober while he gauged whether anyone was studying him. The tavern was preoccupied in the game, following Tommy's lead in jeering Logan, who shook it off with good humor when Rob Clark belted a homerun. Despite the lack of attention, Cal couldn't shake the paranoia that someone would declare him a minor, and although he'd never drunk this much before, with Cass pressing him to think about fathers, he didn't want to stop just yet.

Cass seized the silence to lay into him. "I guess becoming a lush like your mother is *one* way to avoid becoming your father."

Cal knew his frown had to have been pronounced if he could feel his face contort into anything other than his drunken smirk. He found it unfair of Cass to pick a fight with him now. They knew everything about each other, and she'd just demonstrated her willingness to strike him at his deepest fears. Cal knew her well enough to know she was ready to attack another insecurity, and would continue to pounce until he broke. What was worse was that he knew he couldn't respond in kind, as she looked more than willing to escalate this into a shouting match that would get them tossed from the bar, in which case she would have succeeded in cutting him off.

He fantasized about retaliation. Cal plotted calling up Polly (once he'd sobered up) and asking her out. He'd even go out of his way to tell everyone every last detail to ensure word got back to Cass.

He relished the intermission his cell presented when it lit up. Cal ignored the name of the caller the same way he disregarded the number of missed calls displayed on his screen.

"*Where're you?*" a gruff voice demanded.

"Mr. Banks?"

"*Amanda's had to cover for you for over an hour. She's got to pick up her daughter from day care.*"

"Sorry," Cal repented, wincing. "I forgot to call. I—hic—"

"*Christ, are you drunk, kid?*"

It took Cal too long to recognize he was waiting for a response. "No."

"*Geez, kid, you're too young to be tanked.*"

"Mr. Banks," Cal shouted over him, his hoarse voice cracking. "I'm just . . . I'm going through some shit, and—hiccup—"

"*You're fired, kid. That's what you are. I'm sorry, but you've got to learn the hard way, there's a certain level of maturity that's expected in the workplace.*"

Cal didn't want to grovel for his job, not with Cass looming beside him. He didn't want to imagine the level of sanctimony she'd reach if she found out his recklessness had just cost him his job.

"Maybe ending up like Milo really *was* the best you could ever hope for," she shot at him.

He slunk on his stool. "Lay off," he half-heartedly growled at her. "I just wanna go back to the blissful ignorance of yesterday, when we could just spend all day laughing about—"

"We've been busting our asses all year so we can get into good colleges," Cass stated firmly. "We wanted to prove to the world that we were adults, mature enough to handle making decisions about our lives. You shouldn't have skipped school, but at least you could've proved you could make something of your days. What did you do, though, the first time you decided to step out of the confines of our school schedule? You wallowed in aimless self-pity, and capped it off by getting drunk. I'm sure Milo found that freedom of choice daunting, as well. Maybe that's why he cloaked himself in the comforts of predictability.

"I'd be let down if that's all you made of yourself because I always believed you were capable of so much more," she said, and he knew her well enough that even through his hazy vision, he could tell it was becoming an effort to keep her face from crumpling. "But I'd be able to get over that disappointment if that was all you were doing. But what's just . . . absolutely *abhorrent* . . . is watching you give up your dream to not become your father when you know who that really is now, and you know he's so much worse than Milo. That the second you're faced with the possibility you might turn into your *real* father, you don't even muster up an *attempt* to seize control of your life and be better than him.

"I know it must be a mindfuck who your father is. But that shouldn't rattle your belief that you don't have to end up like him, regardless of who he actually is. Nothing's changed. Yet you act like you'll be back here tomorrow, drinking the day away again."

He was grimacing from a bubbling pit of doubt and regret in his stomach that her words had created. Cal hated the way she made everything sound so simple, and refused to admit aloud she was right.

"Maybe I will."

She nodded vigorously, and the bubbling in his gut continued to fester like it had its own pulse while he watched her continue to fight back the tears. "That's just great. Maybe come every day. Don't know how you'll afford it, but go ahead."

"Me, neither. I just got fired," he said, then cringed, wishing he hadn't blurted that out.

Though that finally pushed her to silence, Cal wished it hadn't. Despite the hostilities, it had distracted him from the goings-on of the crowded tavern. There was a chorus of groans, offset by Logan's celebrating, as the Sox fell further behind. Their beloved team was losing, yet everyone was in a jovial mood. It sickened him that they could all be happy while he was suffering, but rather than lash out at them, he directed his ire at Cass.

"Go hang out with Sherman if all you're good for is making people miserable."

He wanted to take it back even before the words left his mouth, and was willing to give anything to rewind time when she responded, "I cancelled plans with him tonight for you."

Cal clumsily reached out to stop her from leaving. He didn't see the elbow she planted in his sternum, only felt the effects that buckled his knees and left him doubled over on his stool. By the time he was able to sit up straight, she was nowhere in sight.

14: Wager

He noticed Chester monitoring him, a frown on his face, cheeks rosy from having had one too many. If he didn't act quick, Cal knew Chester would shuffle over to offer unsolicited advice and philosophies. Drunks like Chester made an art out of cornering anyone who'd listen.

His options for striking up a conversation were limited. Eyes were glued to the television, even though their beloved Sox were down by three runs. The only other topic he could think of that was sure to break the ice with anyone was the identity of his father, and he had no interest in that.

Beside him, Logan and Tommy were drawing the attention of most of the tavern. Even with the crowd noise muffled in his ears, Cal could make out their conversation with some clarity.

"The game's not over until the final out," Tommy insisted. "Let's up the wager—"

The crowd cut him off with an exasperated groan as a double play erased the leadoff walk the Sox had drawn. Tommy hung his head at the latest misfortune.

Cal couldn't help but think he looked natural in that state.

"What'd I tell you?" Logan played to the crowd. They playfully hissed at him, but he just lapped it up. "*This* fool can't help himself. Tommy. *Please*. I beg you. *Stop* making bets with me. I'm starting to feel bad taking your commissions as soon as you earn them."

"Double or nothing," Tommy pronounced.

"No," Logan said, flatly. "Though you may be a fool, you're my friend, and I've no interest in bankrupting you because you can't help making bets, no matter how much you lose. Besides, I'm not a greedy man," he added, with mock humility. "When I win, I spend it here. That's why I try not to take your bets. I'm also not a drunk." Seeing that his comments had drawn a laugh, Logan pretended to sway back and forth, garnering hoots of delight.

Logan's constant guffawing egged Tommy on. "You're just scared you'll finally lose."

That sent the whole tavern into a jubilant uproar, much to Tommy's chagrin.

"What'd I tell you? This fool won't stop until he's paid off my mortgage," Logan exclaimed to the crowd. "What've I got to fear?" he playfully challenged Tommy. "My money's never at risk when you come to me looking for a wager. Remember the four certainties in life," he started to repeat himself.

Tommy's face may have crimsoned with frustration, but Cal was ready to blow. Despite the sucker punch life had thrown him last night, his mind's default reaction to the concept of the future being etched in stone was still to reject it. One rough day hadn't been enough to derail that tendency quite yet. Logan's arrogance spurred Cal to prove him wrong, even if that meant Cass had been right that he could still control his life. Now that she wasn't here, he was willing to entertain the notion that she was right.

Maybe being Vin's son didn't prevent him from walking his own path. Milo had been the prime model of manhood for him growing up, and he'd successfully devoted himself to not following in his footsteps. The lingering dread that his whole life was already mapped out before him festered again, driving him mad to snuff it out.

Cal gave a quick peek toward Chester, saw the boozer was unsteadily rocking off his stool to his feet. Cal swiveled back to the lively discussion, deciding that if he was going to evade Chester's endless ramblings, the time to act was now.

"I'll take the bet," Cal announced, believing Logan would take him up on it since according to him it was easy money, and they weren't friends. Even over the half-hearted enthusiasm they gave to watching the next batter rip a double, the tavern still reacted as though he'd shouted. "How much is the wager?" he asked, thinking this was something else Cass wouldn't approve of.

"Where's your girl?" Logan asked, eyeing the new occupant in the stool next to Cal.

"This *is* the one!" Tommy exclaimed as another batter reached base. "You'll see. If this next guy gets on, Clark'll be up to bat."

Cal was grateful to not have to admit out loud that she wasn't his girl.

Somewhere behind him, Chester, having found his latest victim, began ranting about the decrepit history of the franchise. Cal had a hard time following whether Chester's tirade about management was for drafting Rob Clark over some Kraft kid from Montana, pleading for them to deal Clark while the league felt he had trade value, or griping about how they would end up accepting the worst offer for him, as Chester changed topics at will and with no segues.

Logan continued to study Cal with a puzzled, piercing gaze. "Don't let Tommy convert you," Logan said with a laugh. The smile lingered, but didn't reach his eyes. Those eyes said he didn't want to take money from a kid.

Cal cringed again at the thought that he'd been found out as underage, but it was short lived. The tavern erupted as the Sox hitter singled to load the bases for Rob Clark.

"This is it," Tommy exclaimed, rocking in place.

"I'll bet you it's not."

Tommy's neck snapped toward Cal, taken aback by the challenge. Cal was surprised by his rapid switch in stance as well, and perhaps it was the alcohol taking over, but reversing his gamble made absolute sense to him. The wager was still whether his future was what he made of it. But if he'd been wrong abandoning his belief all day, then he felt he shouldn't be able to profit from having been wrong. If he'd been wrong, he believed he should have to pay the consequences. And deep down, he was willing to pay whatever was necessary to have been wrong.

Tommy regarded his new challenger hesitantly. There may've been a false bravado with Logan, knowing his friend wasn't actually going to take the bet. Now Tommy found himself in a bind, and unable to retreat from his convictions with the whole tavern watching, threw out a number, despite Logan warning him not to flush his entire commission. He frowned when Cal pulled out his wallet.

The broadcast was showing highlights of Clark's game so far as he stepped up to the plate. In addition to being a triple shy of the cycle, the announcers stated he'd gotten a hit every time he swung the bat tonight. But those plate appearances were all early in the game, and this was now the seventh.

Beside him, Tommy was guzzling down his ale, desperately seeking to replenish the fluids now pouring down his forehead. Logan stood resolute, a frown already surfacing. He embodied someone who'd grown weary watching things unfold the same way repeatedly.

There was a collective shout at the screen that the pitch was a foot off the plate. It did nothing to change the umpire's decision to call it a strike. New York's pitcher hurled another slider, also off the plate. The tavern screamed to know what Clark was thinking when he lunged for it, the tip of his bat just making contact with it, fouling it weakly into the stands. Everyone grew quiet as Clark dug in, facing a two-strike count. In a matter of two pitches, Clark's entire demeanor had changed. Cal hadn't thought Clark had been playing with a swagger, but he hadn't resembled anything close to the nervous wreck standing in the batter's box now. Only Tommy looked more anxious.

The pitcher wound up, and flung another slider, this one even farther off the plate. Clark fell over the plate flailing at it, coming up empty.

The mood grew subdued as Tommy was offered condolences. Only Logan clapped Cal on the back to offer congratulations. "What'd I tell you? Some things are inevitable."

"It's . . . " Tommy started feebly. "The game's not over."

Cal had to force a smile. He'd wanted so badly for Rob Clark to prove his critics wrong and come through with a clutch hit, even more than Tommy did. If Rob Clark could change the narrative of his career, Cal's own future wasn't etched in stone. But Clark couldn't even muster a putrid walk, reinforcing Logan's harsh stance on life, one Cal simultaneously refused to accept yet found increasingly difficult to deny. Cal couldn't bring himself to watch any more of it, and ignored the crowd's reactions to the rest of the game.

Cal's vibrating phone snapped him from his depressing daydreaming. His breathing shortened when he saw the call was from "Dad." It took some convincing that it was only Milo, and by that time, the call had gone to voicemail. Cal decided against calling him back, having no idea what to say to the man. Judging by the time, Cal guessed Milo was calling to inquire when he'd be coming home, because he was struggling taking care of Ruby. Milo's check-ins had established a pattern of being placed earlier and earlier in Cal's Friday shifts at the multiplex, but none as early as this. Cal dismissed the notion that Milo knew he'd been fired today.

He nursed his pint, no longer interested in it, but needing something to preoccupy himself. The tavern grew lively as the Sox rallied again in the ninth, within a run, with two on, no one out, and Clark once again stepping up to the plate. Beside him, Tommy clasped his hands together, eagerly watching his hero. Cal pitied him.

"Your phone's going haywire," Paul nodded at the cell as he refilled Cal's pint.

Cal made out the caller's name. "Ugh," he groaned. "It's just my da . . . Milo again, wantin' me to come home. Gawd! It's not even a school night."

"*School night?*"

Cal was still staring dumbfoundedly at his empty hand. He'd just comprehended the pint had been snatched away when he was faced with a new riddle of why the screen was pulling away from him. It wasn't until his back struck the cold pavement that he understood Paul had dragged him out of the tavern.

"Don't ever let me catch you back here again!" Paul barked at him. "Could've gotten shut down because of you!"

"Whaddabout the wager?" Cal called to his back.

The only response was a collective groan followed by "What'd I tell—" before the door slammed shut.

15: Derelicts

Standing was a struggle, and Cal nearly tumbled back down when he stepped on his phone. The screen was cracked. Paul must've thrown it when he'd tossed Cal out of the bar.

He looked around for a taxi. The sidewalk was bobbing up and down before him, making the thought of a trek home daunting. Cal just wanted to collapse into his bed. He'd deal with the hangover tomorrow.

Cal staggered toward a cab across the street, only to watch a small crowd beat him to it. He missed the next two as well, flipping off the taillights of the last cab. He put more distance between himself and the tavern, convinced he'd have less competition getting a cab the farther he got out of the downtown area, but none materialized. Cal stumbled some more until he admitted he was completely lost.

A cough of thunder rumbled ahead. He hadn't noticed the clouds promising rain before now. Biting winds nipped at him. Cal rolled his bleary eyes at his bad luck as he glanced around, trying to decipher which direction would take him back downtown.

"You look cold," an inviting voice beckoned from a nearby alley.

Cal hadn't noticed he'd been shivering, and hugged himself tight to curtail his chattering teeth. He squinted, trying to make out the face the voice belonged to. A warning bell sounded in his foggy brain that it was a bad sign he couldn't see them. Cal shook off the paranoid fear. There was the glow of a trash fire deeper in the alley. The voice wasn't trying to hide something mischievous. His eyesight was just poor from the booze.

"Would you like to join us?" the voice offered.

Cal guessed they'd noticed the fire had caught his attention.

The struggle to concentrate was a feeling Cal remembered from the only time he'd ever been this drunk before. His mind would drift away, tempted by sleep, only to jolt awake, when he'd be momentarily alert before his mind drifted again. Amid the drift, he didn't remember responding, but by the time he'd jolted back to the present, he was standing at the trash fire, joined by the derelicts he'd seen earlier.

"Always with your goddamn plans," Gabs responded to something Randy had said that Cal had missed. She was still working on the cheap rum she'd purchased earlier, and wiped some of what had spilled down her chin. "Miserable life," she sulked. As if accentuating her point, the clouds unleashed the rain.

"You don't know the half of it," Cal replied, too preoccupied inspecting his phone to notice them wince at his blaring voice. The spiderwebs of cracks made the screen impossible to read, let alone call a cab. As he put his cell away, he thought he caught the two sharing a conspiratorial glance.

"For now, I suppose," Randy conceded. "Things'll pick up."

Cal caught himself drifting away again as he stared absently at the embers. When he jolted back, his throat burned from Gabs' bottle, which was now in his hand. He attempted to pass the rum off.

"You keep it," Gabs declined.

"Don't drink," Randy refused.

"Randy still hasn't lost that hardheadedness that led to his ruin," she said, her tone turning nasty. "He just keeps ignorin' all the signs that we were never meant for better. Like how his priors keep George from givin' him a full-time job durin' the summer. Or when Rick—another bum we used to stand around fires with—stole from us the first time we were gettin' money together. Oh, but let's not forget, his *original* scheme to make somethin' of himself, that construction company he ran into the ground."

"It was a mistake leveraging as much credit as I did," Randy agreed. "But losing everything's taught me so much. Just you watch, as soon as I get another chance, I'll be back on top in no time."

"Pah!" Gabs scoffed, spitting again. "You ain't never been on top. You got cut down to the bottom, where you're meant to be."

"I don't believe I'm meant to stay here," Randy stated. "And I don't plan to, either."

"Gabs is right," Cal mumbled, or thought he did. They flinched at his shouting. He pressed on, hoping to stave off the drift he felt coming on. "Life directs you"—he yawned— ". . . where it . . . wants."

Cal knew he was still talking, but like a flickering lightbulb, he began fading in and out of his own speech. He knew he'd started off by stating he'd shared Randy's views of life, but things got hazy quick. He found it likely that he'd brought up his life's mission not to become Milo, because after two years of telling that to anyone who'd listen, it rolled off his tongue. He sprung back into his droning monologue for a few words to hear himself say that life had thrown his plans out the window before drifting back out again, thinking of Vin King, and praying he wasn't spilling that tidbit to them, praying that he was still able to separate his thoughts from what was spewing out of his mouth, and quickly thought about Rob Clark. It wasn't until a siren wailed down the street that Cal became alert again, finding Gabs right beside him, her hand reaching for his pocket.

There was alarm in her eyes, but only for a moment, before she yanked him by the waist to her. "You looked like you were about to fall," she lied smoothly.

"Kid," Randy drew his attention, "whatever they're telling you in school, stop listening. You might look at my life and think dismal futures are inevitable for some of us, but you've learned the wrong lesson. I'm not proof of your outlook on life, you're proof of mine.

"I thought after a few years in construction I could run my own business. I thought I knew it all, too, just because I walked across a stage with a diploma. In short, I was an idiot. Life had much to teach me, and because I was hardheaded, I was forced to learn the hard way. I was just like you, but the key word there is 'was.' I don't drain bottles like you do, not anymore.

You know what that means? I can learn. I can grow. No matter what life does to me, I can improve. You know the one thing it takes to do that?"

Cal shook his head.

"You have to choose to."

Gabs and Randy peered down the alleyway into the street. The siren cut off, but the lights still flashed.

"You look at my misfortunes as life setting things right. But life didn't single me out. What about everyone else who lost their jobs? Or their homes? Or got cancer? Everyone's got shit they've got to face. Christ, look at what happened to that poor Grimes girl. And her father.

"You're taking away the wrong message from life's hardships. Life isn't what happens to you, it's how you respond. I've made a million mistakes. Might make a million more. But as long as I'm still breathing, the only thing about life that's inevitable is that every morning I can decide what to make of that day."

His voice was hypnotic, inviting Cal to drift away again. Cal felt certain he'd entered a dream because he could predict everything Randy said. He knew Randy was preparing to ask for money, and sleepily went through the motions until he heard the amount.

"*Fifty?*" Cal exclaimed, snapping back to reality.

"I know it sounds like a lot," Randy said, casting doubt that Cal had been asleep, "But I swear, I'll put it to better use than you. Better than most anyone. No one understands money's value better than someone who lost all they had."

"Clearly you don't if you're asking for fifty!"

"Listen, kid," Randy started, but Cal felt another strong fade coming on. Cal stuck it out as best he could, but Randy's mesmerizing voice once again entranced him, leaving him uncertain whether he'd drifted off into dreamland. He had a hard time following Randy's rants, if they were even happening. Randy had choice words for governments, who in his opinion understood economics the least, yet were the ones dictating tax rates and where that money went. From the bits and pieces Cal picked up, the tirade then shifted to gripes about the rich squandering their fortunes on frivolous things because they always had an abundance, but showed equal disdain for the low and middle class, because being ignorant of how limitless money's power could be when they got it, they could never appreciate what they had. As best as Cal could make out, the point Randy was driving at was that everyone took for granted how much more they had than him, but if he got a fraction of what they had, he'd surpass them all in no time.

Randy then talked about the newspapers he used as blankets, all the business articles he read, and about this maverick investor who picked gems in penny stocks. His grand plan was to invest in the same companies when the market opened on Monday. Cal jaunted back, about to ask if Randy even had a brokerage account, when he felt his pocket lighten.

"Gabs!" Randy protested. "I had him."

"Pah!" Gabs scoffed. "He wasn't gonna do it."

A searchlight flooded the alley, fixing on the trashcan fire. Cal saw Gabs pull his wallet back defensively as the light caught it. He accidentally clubbed her in the temple with the bottle he'd forgotten he was holding as he clumsily reached for his wallet.

"Oh, fuck you!" she screamed in furious agony, letting go of the wallet to clutch her face.

Cal watched his wallet sail into the darkness of the alley, and didn't react to Gabs' kick until it dropped him. Somewhere off in the distance Cal heard an authoritative voice commanding them all to freeze. Gabs ignored it, and continued kicking.

The last thing he saw was her boot stomping down on his face before everything went dark.

Saturday

16: Lockup

Cal thought he was still dreaming when he found himself in a holding cell. And he thought he was awake when he drifted off into nightmares. His shivering was so pervasive it invaded his dreams, as did his raging gut and splitting headache, blending consciousness and unconsciousness so fluidly he couldn't tell which was which.

It was still dark out the first time he awoke. He slipped back to sleep before he could make sense why he was lying on a bench instead of tucked into his bed. The second time he stayed awake long enough to assess his bruises. He could palm his swollen left eye. His legs were shaky as he stood, and he hobbled to the toilet to vomit. Cal was grateful there wasn't a mirror. He didn't need confirmation that he was an ogre.

Cal had to ease himself back onto the bench. Sleeping on the unyielding lumber had stiffened his back. He had extreme doubts about his ability to fall back to sleep, but was out again in no time.

He wasn't sure if he'd woken up again during the night. Most of his dreams had morphed into him being locked up. Regardless of whether he was awake or not, his one prevailing thought was that he was serving the penance his father had eluded.

Cal thought he was awake when the backs of his eyelids were no longer pitch darkness, but a vibrant red. Light coming from the one barred window in the cell shined down directly where he lay, making it a struggle to open his good eye. He bolted upright when he saw he was now sharing the cell. His body screamed in protest.

"Didn't mean to startle you, son."

Cal clamped his one eye shut, inching his butt along the bench away from m. His head throbbed so angrily he could feel a pulse in his swollen eyelid. This had to be a dream.

"You're not my father," Cal hissed.

His cellmate sighed. Wood moaned, and Cal flinched when he felt the man sit down beside him. Cal convinced himself he'd wake up any minute, but if he opened his eyes before he did, this *would* be real.

"Do you know why I'm visiting you this morning?" the voice asked. Cal remained mute. "Consider me a warning."

"Go away!" Cal screamed.

He accepted this wasn't a dream. None of his hallucinations, vivid as they'd been, had been able to recreate the reek of the vomit he'd missed the toilet with and gotten on his shirt.

"You remind me of myself twenty-five years ago."

Cal cringed when he felt his back being patted. He wanted to shrug off the comforting hand, wanted to spring to his feet, loom over the man, revel for a moment as they cowered before him, before unleashing all his pent-up rage. But he just sat there, allowing himself to be stroked. He didn't have any fight left.

"I'm nothing like you," he sobbed softly.

"We're more alike than you know," the voice said, soothingly. "Had my first beer when I was twelve. Was an alcoholic before my fourteenth birthday. Fifteen was when I started off my weekends with benders. Most people loathed me for being a drunk. Don't blame them. That's what I was.

"Too much of my life was spent having the kind of night you had yesterday. You may've thought it was all good fun, but if you keep it up, you'll regret the memories you were too tanked to remember. It'll tear you up, willing to give anything to get a second chance, knowing you'll never get one."

The voice sniffled hard. "Sometimes . . . I have a hard time remembering what she looked like." The voice paused. "I have to flip through old albums of pictures I don't remember taking. And all I can think is, when did my little girl grow up so fast?"

Cal thought he heard sobbing when the voice paused again.

"I spent my first night in lockup before I graduated high school, too," the voice finally resumed. "I was probably a year younger than you. I wish someone had spoken to me then like I'm doing with you now. I wish someone had tried to reach me before I went through the best years of my life blackout drunk. Because my drinking was only in its infancy when I was a teenager. And if I could find the courage to quit in the face of what happened, I could do it when I was a kid. Maybe I could have more than fading pictures of my girl. Maybe my warnings to stay away from that scoundrel would've been heeded, instead of regarded as irritated drunken ramblings.

"That's why I visit this cell every morning someone your age finds themselves in here. I wasn't saved from suffering and regret, but maybe they can be. At first, I came as a cautionary tale. Don't become me. Now, I hope to serve as inspiration. Everyone in town knows my past. I'm glad they never forget. When they see me on TV every day, I hope they can see how far I've come, and know that if I can turn *my* life around, they can, too."

The wood groaned again, and footsteps whisked across the cell. Cal finally opened his eyes at the sound of jingling keys. A guard was opening the door from the outside.

"Sorry to call you this early," the guard apologized.

"I'll never stop answering the call," he said to the guard before turning back to Cal. Cal wanted to hide his face again, but this time didn't move. "I hope we never meet each other under these circumstances again. You don't want it to come to losing your own Sadie to realize you wasted your life."

He left without another word. The guard studied him for a moment before locking the door. Cal was both relieved and depressed to be alone.

"I'm sorry," he whispered to the emptiness.

Cal sat curled up on the bench, completely immobile, for the longest time. He refused to speak, refused to touch the meal they served. Horrid images came to him from yesterday's haze. None of it felt real, but he had a sense most of it happened. He didn't recognize the monster he'd already become.

Footsteps approached the cell, but Cal didn't budge until he recognized the voice responding to the guard. "Yes, that's him. *Thank* you. We've been worried sick all night."

Cal's head sprang up as Milo entered the cell. "Who's watching Mom?"

"Cass is with her," Milo assured him. "She called me last night to tell me you weren't yourself. I tried calling you first because your mother was having a harsh night, too. By the time I could get someone to look after her and head downtown, you were gone. And I couldn't get hold of you on your phone."

Cal lowered his head. "It's broken. I'm sorry."

"From the fight?" the guard asked from the doorway.

Cal shook his head. "Before that."

"Grady, what's my son charged with?" Milo asked. He'd turned to the guard, and missed Cal cringing at being called his son.

"Nothing. The officers that brought him in first thought he was brawling with two bums, but he's the only one that had any marks on him. They're not pressing charges, either. I think they were grateful they could stay dry last night. We wouldn't've brought him in, but he didn't have any ID on him."

Cal winced. He'd hoped losing his wallet had been a dream.

"I thought he looked familiar, but couldn't place him at first. Then I remembered him from the picture on your desk. Minus the shiner."

Milo nodded. "I'm surprised it was even visible with the mountains of forms and schedules populating my desk this time of year."

"Well, you'll be even busier next year," Grady said, apologetically. "Sarah and I got our returns last week, and when the boys here found out how much we were getting back, they asked who we went with to file."

Cal didn't need to see Milo react to know the added work was already weighing on his mind. He didn't need telepathy either to know he was praying Ruby would be her old self again by next year.

"So, can I take him home?"

Grady nodded, then waved for them to follow. Cal passed Randy, pacing in his cell. "How much longer?" Randy called out to Grady. "I wanna be able to salvage the day and collect *some* cans for the recycling center." He continued to mutter, but all Cal caught was "Monday morning."

Grady led them to the front desk where they were told to wait. Interminable minutes later, he returned with a manila envelope containing Cal's possessions. The only item inside was his cracked phone. They hadn't been able to locate his wallet. Cal doubted he could remember what alley he'd stumbled into last night, and even then, it was sure to be picked clean by now.

For once, he was grateful Milo lacked the ability to find the right words to say. The ride home was mercifully quiet, aside from the white noise from the passing streets. They'd both rolled down their windows once they'd gotten in, to air out the stench of vomit emanating from Cal. Cal nestled his throbbing head against his headrest, utilizing the silence to compose an apology to Cass. No arrangement of words felt suitable.

When Milo pulled into the neighborhood, Cal noticed kids screeching with joy as they stomped and splashed in the puddles. He was so wrought with guilt and depression he couldn't comprehend how anyone could ever experience delight. Cal wished he could relive that level of blissful innocence, just to remind himself what it felt like.

He tensed up when Milo pulled into their driveway. His limbs trembled as the front door opened, only relaxing when Zell emerged. His relief was short lived, swallowed by regret that his comeuppance was being delayed.

"Geez, least tell me th'other guy looks worse," Zell said when he saw Cal. He saw Cal's smile fade as quickly as it was born. He picked up on the question Cal couldn't get past the tip of his tongue. "She had t'get t'work," Zell informed him, before adding in a lower voice. "She's pissed . . . but she wants you t'let her know you're okay."

Cal breathed easier knowing she still wanted anything to do with him. He knew he didn't deserve a second chance after last night. His hands probed the cracked screen of his phone.

Zell frowned, seeing Cal was still glum. "Oh!" he exclaimed as an idea to cheer Cal up burst into his head. "Been dyin' t'tell someone this since yesterday. Had my appointment with Lafia."

Cal gave him a confused look. Nobody looked as ecstatic as Zell did afterward. "Was he . . . *nice*?"

"Not at all," Zell laughed. "First thing he did after skimmin' over my file was hand me applications t'every fast food joint in town. Told me my transcripts painted th'picture that I was hellbent on never earnin' more than minimum wage, and since I didn't put in th'time over the last four years t'improve my grades, he didn't see th'point wasting his tryin' t'help me now."

"And you're . . . laughing about it?"

"Sure am," Zell said, wiping away a tear. "It's as funny now as it was yesterday."

Cal's good eye widened. "You laughed . . . at his advice? At . . . him?"

"Absolutely!" Zell said. He could see Cal's working eye was imploring him to share how Lafia had reacted. "He was furious!" Zell cackled. "Challenged me on th'spot what I'd expected him t'say. So, I tells him with th'reputation he's made for himself, I expected he'd actually offer good advice. You shoulda seen him! Yeah, his mouth was gapin' just like yours, only his face was bright red.

"So, he challenges me again, this time askin' what *I* think I can make of life with my transcripts. So, I tells him how I worked at my dad's auto shop over th'summer, and now work at th'hardware store 'cause they're more flexible with hours. Told him how when I graduate, I'm gonna work full-time for my dad, learn everything 'bout th'business. In th'meantime, I'm getting' t'know everyone I help in th'hardware store, learn what they're comin' in for, makin' recommendations on what contractors are quick, cheap, and do th'best work. Words been gettin' around. Some of them handymen are so appreciative 'bout th'boost in business they've started takin' their trucks t'my dad's when they've needed work. Told Lafia if I kept at it, I'll have a nice little business for myself whenever my dad passes it down t'me.

"I tell ya, his rage was only simmerin' before. He could only stammer for th'longest time. Finally, he manages, real snotty, 'Not surprised you're content never gettin' outta this dinky little town and makin' something of yourself.' He seemed t'think he had me there, and truthfully, I thought he might, too. I don't have th'mind for quick retorts. I was probably more surprised than him when I shot back 'Is that how you see yourself?' He was speechless after that! Left him wheezin' while he grasped for a response. Might've scared th'girl waitin' t'be seen next when she saw me comin' outta his office all smiles. She leaned over t'look past me t'see how he looked. I don't think she saw th'monster she was expectin'."

"She probably got the brunt of his wrath," Cal stated.

Zell shrugged. "And if she did? I keep tellin' y'all, you put too much stock in what Lafia says. His advice had no impact on me. Why should it be th'decidin' factor for any of you?"

Cal's smile lasted longer this time. The sensation of its genuineness surprised him, calling back the echo of a shadow of a memory of feelings he'd had long ago and thought lost forever.

Zell excused himself to head to work. Cal shambled inside to check on his mother. Ruby was still snoring away, though the tossed sheets suggested she'd had as rough a night as him. He frowned, mulling over how much his not coming home last night had contributed to her anxiety.

Cal closed her door and shuffled toward his own bedroom. He felt like walking death, and convinced himself a weekend of sleep was a suitable remedy.

"Cal."

He halted his dragging feet in their tracks. He craned his neck to confirm that Milo had actually spoken. Having never heard a hint of authority from him before, Cal hadn't recognized his voice.

"We need to talk."

17: The Talk

To his surprise, he followed when Milo beckoned. He'd been allowed to change out of his soiled clothes first, and made sure not to dally. Cal felt it unwise to keep Milo waiting. Milo led him through the kitchen into the living room to put as much distance between them and Ruby. When Milo gestured for Cal to close the doors behind them, Cal obeyed. He eyed Milo curiously the whole time, wondering if Milo had been keeping this commanding aspect of his personality buried his whole life.

"What's gotten into you?" Milo asked in his usual soft-spoken manner.

The bluntness coming from Milo caught him off guard, and before he caught himself, Cal responded in kind. "I know."

He winced, knowing he'd flubbed how he'd wanted to approach the subject. After a day possessing the knowledge, Cal realized he'd done everything imaginable to avoid thinking about how to bring up the topic of his father, but he knew this wasn't it. He didn't need to see befuddled eyes staring back at him to recognize Milo wasn't following.

"My father," was all Cal could get out before getting choked up. The emotions he'd tried suppressing burst through the dam, swallowing him in its tidal wave.

"Cal, I'm your father."

Cal sobbed. Milo must not know, he thought, then felt overridden with guilt that he, another man's son Milo had been duped into raising, was going to be the one to reveal his mother's betrayal to him. Cal didn't believe Milo would take this in stride like he'd done with everything else life threw at him. He was going to evict them, divorce Ruby, leave her with nothing except the souvenir she'd gotten from another man. Cal wouldn't blame him.

Cal shook his head. "You don't understand."

"I'm your father," Milo repeatedly firmly.

Cal writhed in agony as the tears rained down. He didn't want to hurt this man, but he didn't know how to break the news gently.

"Mom . . . she . . . she went—"

For the first time, Milo grew impatient. "Cal, I don't care who you got your genes from. I'm your father."

Cal's snivels cut themselves short. Milo sat there silently, allowing Cal to study him while processing what Milo had just said. Cal was grateful Milo was willing to wait patiently until he was ready to speak again. It was odd to experience Milo knowing the right thing to do in these moments.

"You . . . know? About me?"

"Of course. I agreed to it."

The response led to more silence. Time crawled by as Cal tried to comprehend this new information.

"You were okay with that? Raising another man's child?"

"Should I be worried he might come back into the picture?" he asked, flashing a smirk.

Cal smiled back for a moment. It'd been awhile since Milo had attempted a joke, and he'd have to think way back to recall one that was actually funny.

"But . . . why?"

"Because I love your mother. I have since before I even understood that I loved her. I first met her in second grade. She was the first girl I ever offered my cookies to at lunch, and I loved it every time she accepted. I even got your grandma to buy different kinds when I found out Ruby's favorites."

Cal suspected he had a lifetime of stories like these to tell, but knew Milo needed to move along. Cal found himself hoping to hear them someday.

"We didn't date in high school. Vin beat me to that. I hated seeing her with him, but I didn't think it'd be such a big deal. Everybody knew he swapped girlfriends pretty quickly. But he stayed with her, as her husband I can see why, and she stayed faithful to him even after he enlisted."

Cal nodded.

"My friends all thought I was nuts. They told me there were billions of other girls out there. They told me to find another one, because she'd given her heart to Vin. They suggested I move far away to purge Ruby from my memory." He shrugged. "I just kept telling them she was the one. It wouldn't be fair entering a relationship with another I felt I was 'settling' for. My friends really ramped up their efforts of . . . persuasion . . . when Vin was killed. They concluded she'd never love another as deeply as she'd loved him. The state she's in now isn't anything new. She was catatonic like this for years. The drinking's made it worse this time around.

"Most thought I was foolish when I tried courting your mother in that state. Only a handful of her friends pushed her to go on dates with me just to get her out of the house, and I don't think they saw me as her soulmate, but as a reminder of what happiness could feel like."

"Did she . . . was she . . .?" Cal stammered, failing to find a gentle way to pose his question.

Milo shook his head. "It wasn't like a switch turned on and she was cheerful again. She occasionally smiled on our early dates, but she frowned most of the time."

Cal felt *himself* frowning. He couldn't wrap his head around why Milo continued to ask his mother out when she'd been giving him every indication she wasn't interested.

Milo seemed to read his mind. "Cal, when you love someone, you don't just abandon them because they hurt your feelings. I've never denounced you as my son, have I?"

Cal lowered his head in shame as he reflected on all the ugliness he'd directed toward Milo. The man had always taken it in stride, and always treated each new day as though the hostilities from yesterday had no lingering effects.

"I realized I'd been going about things the wrong way with Ruby. I'd been incredibly selfish, feeling that Vin's death was a situation I could capitalize on to be with the woman of my dreams. I'd never stopped to consider she might not be ready for another relationship. We had an open and honest discussion about us. I told her she could never scare me away if she ever wanted to offload any of the heartache she was carrying around inside. I suggested we could attend couple's counseling, or if she'd be more comfortable, individual therapy sessions. I even offered to pay for her appointments, no strings attached, even if she told me the relationship wasn't working. I just wanted to see her get better.

"That was the scariest moment of my life. I'd waited years for my chance with Ruby, and not only was I on the verge of losing her, I was willingly giving her up. But our relationship was all wrong the way it was. It didn't matter how many dates we'd gone on, I didn't have her heart, and would never get it if I kept at it the way I'd been. I knew the only way to fix things was to let her go and trust she'd want to come back to me.

"I could barely eat or sleep for two days. But as agonizing as those days were, it was all worth it when she said she wanted to give couple's counseling a try. We were easily the couple with the shortest relationship our therapist had ever counseled with only a few months of dates under our belt, but given Ruby's past, it was right for us.

"That's the moment she started becoming receptive to my love. I've never been a Casanova. If my suaveness was pitted against Vin's, I'd lose in a landslide. But I more than made up for it with compassion, something Vin always lacked. You don't have to look any further than his own mother. The reason he'd given for his sudden enlistment after Sadie's disappearance had been to help his mother raise his siblings, but he never even called her once he'd left. I think Ruby finally saw her happiness was my genuine concern. Going by what Vin's former flames have divulged about their relationships, I doubt she got this level of empathy from him."

Cal nodded, but the concerned look on his face never left. Milo had related the story of how Ruby had fallen in love with him, but that didn't explain why he wasn't Cal's biological father. When he turned to Milo, Cal found him waiting patiently. He realized Milo understood this was a lot to process, and had chosen to wait until Cal indicated he was ready to hear more.

"After we were married, we tried having children. Unsuccessfully. Your mother was distraught she might be barren. I was actually relieved when it turned out *I* was the problem. We considered adoption. We even had most of the paperwork filled out. It was while we were gathering everything for the background check that Ruby found some old keepsakes from when she'd dated Vin. Gifts, letters—"

"I've seen them," Cal interrupted, not wanting to relive the experience of finding them.

Milo relented. "He'd donated sperm to a fertility clinic to pay for a date once. I can't say I loved hearing my wife's proposal to become impregnated by a former lover, nor the look in her eye when she pitched it. She suddenly looked and acted like she was on the verge of slipping back into her deep depression if the possibility of capturing a slice of the future she'd lost with Vin was denied to her a second time. Truth be told, while I wanted a child with her, adoption, it . . . I felt like I was compromising. At least this way, we'd be raising *her* child. And it brought you into my life. I've always felt it was a fair trade."

"Weren't you ever worried about what people around town would think about you when they found out you were raising another man's child?"

Milo shrugged. "No more than if we'd followed through on adoption."

Cal's pupils ran their familiar lap in their sockets. "It's not the same thing and you know it. Couples adopt children all the time. What you and Mom did had to have sounded crazy to people."

"Cal, the only ones who know are a nurse, doctor, and receptionist in another state and everyone under this roof."

Cal's mouth hung agape as he attempted over and over again to compose a response before surrendering to speechlessness. He thought about how much it must have terrified Milo to stray that far from his hometown, and how much Ruby's happiness, as well as Milo's own desire for a family, must have meant to his father to follow through with it anyway. And even when Milo's decision to step outside his comfort zone turned his life upside down almost two decades later, Milo never cried foul.

Cal put himself in Milo's shoes for the first time, reflecting on the disarray that had taken place under their roof since Vin King had been linked to Sadie Grimes' murder. Milo came home from a grueling day at work to find his wife had sunken into a deeper and darker misery, only to be berated by a brat who wasn't even his child, and because no one knew the truth regarding Ruby's pregnancy, he had no one to confide in.

He'd never once bemoaned his situation. He never lashed out at Ruby for how unfairly his kindness had been twisted against him. He'd passed on every opportunity to respond to Cal's constant harassment. It could've been so easy for him to combat Cal's constant belittlement with the revelation of who his real father was. Instead, Milo allowed the entire weight of the family secret to be placed on his shoulders, knowing there would be no one to turn to for help.

This knowledge made Cal see how wrong he'd been about Milo. He couldn't believe he'd ever entertained the thought that Milo was meek. His father's bravery to face this alone made Milo the strongest man he'd ever known.

"But . . . ." Cal's voice trailed off as he searched for the right words. "You never found it the cruelest torture looking at me every day, seeing me grow into the man Mom loved?"

"You're not growing into anything you're not choosing to. You had no problem believing you had complete control not turning into me."

Hearing his words repeated back to him hit Cal hard. He was now ashamed by how proud he'd been going above and beyond in pursuit of his desires. Cal knew it'd been childish behavior, but he could finally see how far he'd been from the adult he'd demanded to be treated as.

"That was before I found out who . . . not my 'real' one . . . but who my biological dad was." His mind grew heavy with guilt as he reflected over his behavior, and he dropped his penitent eyes to the floor again, believing himself unworthy to look Milo in his.

"Drinking wasn't the only bad thing I did yesterday," he confessed. "I socked someone at school. I wasn't thinking, I was angry and I just did it. It's scary to think that's where my thoughts went to the first time I didn't care what happened and let my base instincts takeover."

"Is that what you're worried about?"

Cal looked up to see Milo wearing a concerned frown. "You can stop that nonsense right now because I can tell you you're not Vin."

"Dad, I also—"

"I'm sure you can give me a laundry list of evil deeds you've done yesterday. And we'll discuss appropriate punishments later."

Cal nodded. Any sentence would be fair.

Milo smirked.

"What?" Cal asked.

"It's just amusing. You don't even realize you've proved the point I'm about to make."

Cal stared back at Milo, confused.

"The moment I mentioned repercussions, you accepted them without protest. Does that sound like Vin King to you?"

Cal shook his head. A ray of relief poked through the hefty cloud of guilt he harbored within.

"I'm disappointed you got into a fight yesterday," Milo went on, "but you didn't try to hide it. You probably could've kept mute about it until you were no longer living under this roof, and I would've never known, but you came clean about it. On your own. That sounds nothing like devising a plan to flee town and never return.

"It's only natural to look back and focus on all the horrible things we've done in life. But when you're a parent, you possess this unwavering ability to see the good in your children. Even when they stumble. Especially when they're at their lowest. Would it be fair to say yesterday was the worst day of your life?"

He waited for Cal to nod. "And yet, even at your lowest, the first thing you did when you saw me was ask who was taking care of Mom. Then you apologized for inconveniencing me. If you think you're destined to become Vin King because you share some DNA with him, would you have showed any of that compassion so readily, any of that empathy at all? There are millions of things that make you nothing like the man. And if you ever for a second think you've no choice but to follow in his footsteps, I'll list every one of them."

Cal felt ready to dance on clouds each time Milo spoke. The dark fog of guilt that had festered within him had all but dissipated in the face of Milo's positivity. There was still one thing that nagged him.

"What about you and Mom? You described courting her like you were helpless to do anything but love her," Cal played devil's advocate. "Why should I be gifted with choice when you weren't."

"But I *did* have a choice," Milo explained. "I might've had no say in who I fell in love with, but remember, it wasn't until I expressed absolute selflessness, willing to give her up if that's what was best for her, that she was finally able to see how deep my affection ran for her. And I was rewarded many times over. Because when I did, what everyone thought was impossible happened. She finally moved on from Vin King. So, if I could be gifted with choice, why can't you?"

Once again, Cal was left contemplating how wrong he'd been after hearing his own words repeated to him. Something still badgered him. "She still has a box of keepsakes from Vin." He wasn't sure how Milo would take the news, but believed he had a right to know.

"I know," Milo said. "We decided to keep them. We weren't sure if we'd ever tell you about your biological father, but if we did, we wanted to present you with some evidence of the type of man he'd been. Obviously, we had no idea who he really was until recently.

"You may know about her keepsake box, but you don't understand why she revisits the past." He sighed, and for the first time, looked unsure of how to proceed. Clarity entered his eyes, as though the stumble had given him the solution. "You've accused me of not knowing how to help Ruby. Would you say this talk has been helpful?" Cal nodded. "Do you find that surprising?" Cal grimaced, but nodded again. "It's because I've gotten plenty of practice over the last few months. You're going through the same thing as your mother. Grief over the truth. She's been combing through her old love letters looking for any clues about the monster she once loved. She imposes harsh sentences on herself for even proposing to raise his child. She insists on serving penance, and grows nasty when I tell her none of this was her fault. Ruby thinks she ruined all our lives by forever linking us to Vin. She doesn't regret her decision to have you, she can't help but love you. But she loathes the details within that decision."

Cal shuddered at the notion that she might see Vin King when she looked at him. He'd done nothing over the past months to dissuade her of that opinion. This whole time he'd placed the blame for her misery squarely on Milo's shoulders. Like everything else, now he understood the truth.

A tiny voice inside his head echoed the memory of his declaration that he would find a way to help his mother. He now knew what that entailed. There *was* something he could do about the DNA he shared with Vin King.

He could consider it irrelevant.

Cal resolved to himself he would refuse to become his father.

18: Fixing Ruby

Cal spent hours composing an apology to Cass, as he made sure to include all the things that had gone unsaid until now. By far the longest text he'd ever written, he still found it inadequate. He would've had an easier time drafting an email, but he'd wanted her to see it immediately.

Cal decided not to disturb Milo by returning his phone while he was in his study working through another weekend. His eyes took some time adjusting to the world again after spending so long staring at the phone screen. He was surprised the sun was still out. The day felt a month old.

He thought some fresh air would do him good. Cal was startled to find Jamie waiting on his stoop when he stepped outside. The sophomore looked ready to apologize for spooking him, then for gawking at his bruises, but nothing came out.

"It's good to know you don't think my face is an improvement," Cal said with a shrug.

Jamie's face broke into a smile. The levity put him at ease enough to speak. "Milton didn't do that, did he?" he asked, pointing to Cal's black eye.

"No, and I don't think he'll be seeking me out, either," Cal assured him. "It looks worse than it feels."

Jamie nodded. Cal suspected the kid believed he was lying, but appreciated the attempt. It became an effort for him to speak again. "I just . . . wanted to tell you . . . I really appreciated you stacking," he cut himself off to clap his hands over his mouth, "*sticking* up for me. No one's ever done that before."

"That punk only picks on you because he sees you by yourself. Why don't you sit at our lunch table on Monday? I guarantee he won't bother you."

"Sure!" Jamie exclaimed. It was the first time Cal had ever seen him as anything besides anxious and morose. Jamie also looked taller, no longer bearing the weight of the world on his shoulders. It was the first time he'd seen Jamie stand up straight. Jamie's face quickly settled back into its usual glum expression, though. "I'm going to have to bring all my books back to school."

Cal shrugged. "I can help. I left everything at school, so my hands will be free." The grateful, excited look returned. "Why'd you clean out your locker anyway?"

"So my mom wouldn't have to." His hands shot to his mouth again. Cal had never seen anyone look so embarrassed. He wasn't even sure what Jamie had accidentally flubbed this time.

"Well, either way, stop by if you need me." Jamie slowly uncovered his mouth, looking beyond grateful that Cal wasn't dwelling on what he'd said. "See you Monday?"

Jamie mulled it over for a bit. Then he flashed a smile that Cal sensed he'd rarely showcased. Its awkwardness made it charming. "I'll be there."

He'd never seen Jamie carry himself with such confidence as he strutted back home. Cal stood there watching him disappear from view before heading inside.

Ruby had finally emerged from the bedroom and was rummaging through the linen closet. "Why'd everything in my life become tainted?" she mumbled in frustration as she searched between the multicolored towels. "All because I was foolish enough to love him." She retrieved a rosé buried under a stack of bedsheets when she realized she was being watched. Ruby spun around with a remorseful look to see her son had caught her red-handed.

"You don't need that, Mom," he said. With a little effort, he was able to pry it from her hands. "Trust me, it'll be easier to get through what's bothering you without this," he said, giving the bottle a slight wave. His head throbbed slightly, serving as a reminder of his own failed efforts to sidestep his pain.

"Oh, it's no good!" she cried, brushing past him. "I'll be depressed forever."

He followed her into the living room, where she plopped down on the floor up against a sofa. She curled up into a sitting ball, burying her head in her kneecaps.

"Mi—Dad says you've been like this before I was born." He winced seeing her stiffen, but knew he had to press on. "Haven't you been happy since you had me?"

"Oh, my sweet prince, of *course* I have been!" Her soaked eyes shot up from her kneecaps to meet his, their intensity begging him to believe her. "You're one of the few beacons of light I've got in this . . . it's tough to describe . . . it's like . . . like . . . a bottomless pit of sad."

"It can't be bottomless," he said, taking a step toward her, doing his best to ignore how much it hurt seeing her retreat as much as the sofa allowed. "You climbed out of this before."

Her head bobbed. It took a moment for it to occur to Cal she was weeping. The lack of fresh tears had made it difficult to tell. She'd shed so many over the past months, it was as though her body couldn't produce anymore.

"My prince, it's like the universe has conspired to spoil my life. I don't know what I did to deserve such cruelty. I dread I'm doomed to one million days of this suffering."

She buried her head into her kneecaps again, too busy sobbing to notice him inch closer. Ruby didn't realize he'd sat down until she recoiled when he put his arm around her.

"What're you doing?"

Cal shrugged his free shoulder as he held her tight to him. "A million days . . . it's long," he conceded. "But, it's not forever. I'll wait here with you so we can be happy again the moment you're ready."

Ruby remained rigid in his embrace for the longest time as her eyes studied him. Cal merely patted her shoulder reassuringly while she did. Finally, she tentatively lowered her head until it rested on his shoulder. He couldn't see her face, but he was sure he felt her brimming smile against his chest.

"You're just like your father," she whispered warmly.

Cal smiled. "I know."

Enjoyed I'm Not My Father

Thanks for joining Cal Fisher on his path toward self-discovery. If you enjoyed his journey, please leave a review on Amazon as it helps other readers discover his story

Author's Note

This is a work of fiction. Names, characters, places and incidents either are products of the author's imagination or are used fictitiously, and any resemblance to any persons, business establishments, or locales is entirely coincidental.

More books written by Damian Myron

Dig Down

Betrayed by his friends and clients, Rob Moore finds himself implicated in the explosive scandal of a tarnished Congressman. Aware these same friends were behind the Congressman's execution, and want to silence him in the same manner, his only option is to run for his life. But how long can he evade compromised cops, ruthless businessmen, a merciless mobster and the sadistic cartel?

Lock the Doors

Reclusive Bobby Dinwill comes home after a fruitless day of fishing to find an unfamiliar van parked in front of his lakeside cabin. When he hears voices appraising the value of his possessions, he realizes the strangers are already inside.His first thought is to run however many miles it takes to get to the nearest neighbor. Before Bobby can take his first step, his alarm goes off, reminding him he's already late taking his medication. His terrified eyes back turn back to his cabin, where he left his supply of pills that morning.

Acknowledgments

I'd like to offer a special thanks once again to my editor, Dorrie O'Brien, for continuing to work with me to shave away all the raw edges of my ideas and craft them into the vision I always had for them.

About the Author

Damian Myron was educated at Siena College. He is the author of two other novels, *Dig Down* and *Lock the Doors*, and a collection of short stories, *Dig Down Accessories*. He spends most of his time day dreaming of other worlds.

www.ingramcontent.com/pod-product-compliance
Lightning Source LLC
Chambersburg PA
CBHW052000220626
47052CB00004B/1030